P9-CDI-026

DISCARD.

PARCHED

PARCHED

❖ ❖ ❖

MELANIE CROWDER

HARCOURT
Houghton Mifflin Harcourt
Boston   New York

Copyright © 2013 by Melanie Crowder

For information about permission to reproduce selections
from this book, write to Permissions,
Houghton Mifflin Harcourt Publishing Company,
215 Park Avenue South, New York, New York 10003.

Harcourt is an imprint of
Houghton Mifflin Harcourt Publishing Company.

www.hmhbooks.com

LIBRARY OF CONGRESS CATALOGING-IN-PUBLICATION DATA
IS AVAILABLE.

ISBN 978-0-547-97651-8

Manufactured in the United States of America
DOC 10 9 8 7 6 5 4 3 2 1
4500407166

R0452564305

For Whitney

NANDI

�֍ ✳ ✦

I

Sniff-sniff. My tail parts tall grass, swish-swish.

Bright sun up. Heat sizzle in air.

I jog. My head swings side-side. The pups waddle, stumble over too-long legs, too-big feet.

Sarel-girl runs with me, hand on my neck, hair flap-flap in wind, feet slap-slap on dirt. Pups nip her skinny ankles. She makes laughter sound of wood hoopoe bird: *khee-hee-ee khee-hee-aa-aa-aa.* Sarel-girl swats Chakide on rump. Lifts face to wide sky. Makes bird sounds some more.

Rumbles in dirt. I stop. Head up, I sniff side-side. Engine sound from sun-up side. Black snake tires spin up dust.

My tail stiff. Pups smell now, sniff-sniff, sniff-sniff-sniff.

Pups whine. I growl. Pups lie bellies to dirt, ears up, eyes wide.

Sarel-girl kneels. I show teeth, stand over girl. She lies belly to dirt. No bird sounds now.

We watch through tall grass.

Fear scent.

Man-with-whistle stands in front of house, hands up. Ibubesi, Ubali at side, hackles up. Show teeth.

Men running, pointing house, pointing kennel, pulling buckets out of well. Shouting, kicking empty buckets.

Pack in kennel angry bark, fear bark. Let-me-out bark.

Men lift black sticks, shouting.

Crack-crack-crack.

Ibubesi jumps, falls to ground. Makes hurt whine.

Man-with-whistle falls, face to ground.

Blood scent.

Woman-in-window runs out of house onto dirt.

Crack-crack-crack.

Woman-in-window flies up in air, lands flat on back.

"Mama!" Sarel-girl yells.

I snarl. Sarel-girl gets up on hands, on knees. I step on shoulders, push girl belly to dirt. Sarel-girl makes angry sound, fear sound. LOUD. I hold back of neck with teeth. I growl, soft.

Thando licks salt drips from her face.

Fire scent. Crackle sound.

Engine sound. Black snakes on dirt, spinning dust.

Death scent.

MUSA

✤ ✤ ✤

2

Scraps of plywood covered every gap in the rusted walls. A rat scampered across the sloping roof. It was quiet in the dim room, except for the sound of shallow breathing.

A key scraped in the lock and the door swung inward, spreading a rectangle of yellow light across the floor. A boy huddled in the corner, his face buried in the crook of an arm. Flies landed on seeping scabs at his wrists and ankles.

Sivo crossed the dusty floor, his steel-toed boots tramping out the sound of the boy's breath.

"That's him. That's the dowser," Sivo said to the guard waiting in the shadows of the doorway. A scar cut across his cheek and over his lips, pulling at his mouth when he spoke.

"Musa," Sivo said. But the boy didn't move, even at the sound of his name. "Get up."

Sivo bent to undo the padlock at Musa's ankles, and the boy flinched, the chains around his wrists clanging against each other.

Sivo clipped a leather leash onto the links between Musa's wrists and yanked him up, dragging him outside. The guard in the doorway backed out of reach, lifting a hand to cover his nose as they passed.

Outside, Musa closed his eyes against the glare of the midday sun and raised his face to the sky. The rubber toe of his canvas shoes flapped open with each step. A drop of sweat slid down the ridges of his bare spine. He almost made it to the jeep, but he stumbled on a rock jutting out of the hard dirt. Sivo yanked him upright with a sharp tug on the leash.

Musa crawled into the back seat.

He lay unmoving, his eyes crimped shut. The jeep rocked as the men climbed in and slammed the doors. As soon as the engine rattled to life, Musa curled into a ball, gathering his bleeding wrists to his chest. The pain that flared up his arms and legs was always at its worst in these moments, when a breeze washed over his broken skin, when the sun glinted off the links of the chains that held him. When life out of that dusty shack, and away from the Tandie, hovered at the edges of his sight.

The city streets were clogged with rusted-out cars stripped of their tires and tilting at odd angles. Only two men walked the streets under the glaring sun, their black hair matted with dust and their lips cracked and bleeding. They stared at the jeep as it passed, its blaring music fading out of tune as it rattled down the street.

After winding and bumping through the ruined roads for nearly an hour, the jeep stopped. Musa lurched in the back seat, barely catching himself from spilling onto the floor.

Sivo stepped out and threw open the back door, shaking a ring of keys as he leaned over the boy.

Dangling off the edge of the seat, Musa slid to the ground. He swayed on his feet, the weight of the chains bowing his thin shoulders.

"No funny business," Sivo said as he bent to undo the padlock holding Musa's hands together.

Musa clenched his teeth as the chains grated

against the sores on his wrists. There was a click, then the clanking of falling metal. His arms fell to his sides, and blood rushed to fill his fingers.

"What you waiting for, boy?"

"Thirsty . . ." Musa whispered.

"That's what we're here for, ya?" Sivo said, his hands bent backwards on his hips. When Musa didn't move, Sivo reached into the jeep and pulled out a dusty water bottle, its sides nicked with small white creases.

He held the bottle upside down at arm's length and squeezed a stream into the boy's mouth. The water was warm and tasted like the plastic drum it had been stored in for months. Musa swallowed, the back of his tongue clicking against the roof of his mouth for long moments after the stream of water had stopped. An ache rose in his belly and his jaw fell slack.

"That's it. Go on." Sivo shoved a pair of thin forked sticks into Musa's chest.

Musa's arms folded over them. He turned and scuffed away from the jeep. With a stick clasped in each hand, he lowered his forearms until they stuck out from his body like a long-legged insect.

He closed his eyes, and listened.

S A R E L

✤ ✤ ✤

3

Sarel woke, screaming.

The sound bounced off the walls of the underground room. She lay in a curve of bony knees and
elbows, the mortared stones of the grotto floor carving dents into her flesh. Her body sagged, sapped. Her
eyelids quivered with memories that kept her from
sleeping.

Sarel clutched at her throat, raw from smoke and
screams and hot tears. Her skin was smeared with soot.
When she blinked, ash drifted down onto her cheeks.
Under heavy lids, her eyes, the color of a tide pool
stirred by a storm, stared at the stones. Flat. Empty.

Thirteen black-mouthed dogs spilled down the

curving stairs and pooled on the pebbled floor all around her. The air, still laced with smoke, hung heavy in the small, round room.

Sarel uncurled, her mind slow with things like how she had gotten there and why she was lying on the ground, a weight as heavy as stones pressing into her chest and shoving the air from her lungs.

Nandi stood over her, sniffing at her breath and licking the soot from her face. Watching Sarel as if she were one of her own pups, skittish and stunned.

Sarel hadn't risen from the grotto floor since the flames had leaped from the roof of the house to race through the tinder grasses, chasing her away from the twisted, still bodies of her parents. Chasing her to this underground place of quiet, and cool stones, and pooled water.

The sound of agony, of labored breathing and crushing pain, filled the small room. Sarel set her breath by it, and she opened the ache in her chest to it.

The sound inched closer. It echoed against the curved walls. It pressed against her, nuzzled at her. It cut through the blur in her mind and laid the memories bare.

Sarel clamped her hands against her ears, against

the shouting, the gunshots, the sound of the dogs baying in their kennel. She squeezed her eyes tight. Shut out the sight of her father's body soaking the ground with blood, of her mother's hands, limp, still coated with a dusting of flour.

The memory was gone as quickly as it came, leaving Sarel gasping for air. She curled back into herself, and a wail rose in her throat.

When Sarel woke again, the sound was still there, but softer and pitched higher. She sat up, blinking. Nandi lay beside her, watching, waiting. Sarel lifted a hand to graze the underside of Nandi's jaw. The pups pressed in close, ears pricked, tails tucked between their legs. They nipped at Sarel's ankles and licked her unresponsive face.

But that sound—it was more than the whimpers of thirsty pups.

Sarel twisted to face it.

On the other side of the grotto pool, Ubali lay on his side, panting, each breath a cry of pain. Sarel crossed the pebbled floor on her knees and leaned over him. She drew her fingers along the velvety tip of his ear. His tail thumped once, but he didn't try to lift his head.

Sarel's eyes skittered to a knuckle-size hole in Ubali's shoulder that leaked maroon blood onto the stones beneath him. She yanked back her hand.

The word formed on her tongue, and she curved her lips around it.

Bullet. She had to get the bullet out.

Panic came in rapid-fire breaths, scraping against her throat and pounding into the weight that crushed her lungs. She couldn't do this. Not by herself.

Teeth gripped her arm, startling, steady. Nandi held Sarel's forearm between her jaws, her eyes clamped onto the girl's stricken face. Sarel gulped in air until her breath slowed, until the pounding in her head faded.

She lifted her eyes to the pebbled ceiling and pressed two fingers into the wound, digging, probing, slipping in the place where blood met bone.

Ubali's cries slackened.

With a gasp, Sarel hooked her finger around a lump of metal. Wincing, she pulled the bullet up and out. It fell to the stones, slick with blood.

Ubali lifted his head off the ground and grunted, twisting his neck to lick the wound clean.

Sarel stared at her hands. They were covered with

blood that clung like webs between her fingers. She would have to go up and scrub them in the sand until they were scraped clean. Up where the air was still heavy with soot. Up where the bodies of her parents lay in the charred dirt.

Nandi crossed to the stairs and waited.

Sarel followed, her bloody hands stretched out in front of her.

MUSA

❖ ❖ ❖

4

Musa walked across the empty lot, pushing bursts of pebbles and silt in front of him with each step. Back and forth he shuffled, like a pointer flushing birds out of tall grass. The sticks in his hands stretched out into the air before him and ticked slowly side to side.

Halfway down the stretch of packed dirt, the sticks swung together, crossing his chest and slapping against his sweat-streaked skin. Musa stopped and scraped a line in the dirt with the rubber toe of his shoe. He listened for any sign of water below, for the buzz that settled in the base of his skull whenever fresh water was near.

Nothing.

Still he followed the way of the dowsing sticks, backing up, moving a pace to the left, and stepping forward again. When the sticks crossed in front of his body a second time, Musa etched another line in the dirt.

Sivo pushed off the jeep, spitting out the straw he'd been rolling between his teeth, eyes intent on the boy's shuffling progress.

Back and forth, back and forth. The line of hatch marks stretched straight across the dirt.

Too straight.

Musa paused and squinted up and down the line. He closed his eyes, listening. The hairs on his arms lifted off his skin and he bit a corner of his lip, letting it slide through his teeth. The place where his tongue had touched glared red against the rest of his dust-coated skin. His hands fell to his sides, the thin sticks bending as they brushed against the ground.

Nothing.

His head bobbed on his neck, too heavy to hold upright.

"Well?" Sivo shouted.

Musa shook his head. He took a few wobbling steps away from the line of dead water.

Sivo stomped after him. "And that's all you're good for? A map of every bladdy sewer line in this city?"

Musa cringed. He lifted the sticks to begin again, the scarred skin over his shoulders twitching and rippling.

NANDI

�֍ �֍ �֍

5

Ibubesi, Thembo, Ganya, all gone.

Flames chased impala, spiral-horned kudu, spring hares far from this place with smoke in air. Far from this all-death place.

Bheka and Icibi go to sun-down side. Go where ground is not all burnt. Hunt.

I stay.

Pups whine, noses in dust, sniff-sniff. Paw at blood scent in ground, scratch-scratch. Whine for Thembo, for Ganya, for Ibubesi. For Man-with-whistle.

I stay with Ubali. With Sarel-girl. She does not come out under sun. She lies on stones. Lost in screaming place.

I watch sun-down side.

I wait for Bheka and Icibi to bring food. Wait for Sarel-girl to wake from screaming place.

SAREL

✤ ✤ ✤

6

It was the dogs who got Sarel up off the grotto floor, who washed the dreams from her face and nibbled at the weight pushing her down.

She felt like the paper-thin husk of a golden berry, ripped apart and trampled underfoot. The pain in her throat and her belly, the angry press of her blad-der — she could ignore those things. But she couldn't bear the pups' thirsty whines.

They were her father's dogs. Sarel had watched while he trained them, had pattered after him while he checked their paws, their gums, their muscled gait. They weren't just livestock, bred and sold and bred again, not to him.

Not to Sarel either.

They were ridgebacks. Lion hunters. Prized for their fierceness and their fearlessness. They could protect themselves, feed themselves. And they would protect her, now that she was all alone.

But they needed her too.

There was no water left up there. Not anymore.

Ripples in the earth and the half-buried shells of long-dead water creatures were the only sign that creeks and marshes had once streamed between the dry riverbeds.

Sarel rolled herself off the ground. She gripped the pump handle jutting out of the wall beside her and hefted it up, then down, up, then down, leaning her belly into the grooved steel to coax the water up and out. After a half-dozen tries, water chortled out of the pipes, splashing into the shallow pool and turning the ash-colored stones green and black and deep purple. The dogs rushed forward to lap up the water.

Sarel watched them drink, running her hands over the pebbled walls, tracing the spiral of stones that surrounded the water spout. Her fingers slowed as a wary thought lodged itself in her mind.

The men with the guns—this was why they came

to the homestead. They were looking for the secret store of water that had sustained the family while the drought sucked the life out of every other living thing.

They had been searching for the old well. But they hadn't known to look past the house, to a ring of stones at the back of the yard. They hadn't known that the stones marked the place where steps curved down into a cave under the ground, with a pump and a small pool set into the far end. A pump that was fed by the deep well Sarel's grandfather's grandfather had dug out of the earth when he first settled the land.

The men with the guns and the blood-red flags hadn't known to look for a grotto; they didn't even have the word for such a thing. A grotto belonged in a land where brine and mist filled the air, where water spilled over into every solid space.

Not here. Not in this place of dust and death.

There was nothing in Sarel's stomach, but still she retched, a sob slipping through the bile on her tongue.

The singed hem of her cotton shirt bunched up her back as she slid to the floor. Her hands fell limp into her lap. Her skin was burned brown as the bark of a guarri tree from years under the fierce sun. Scrapes covered her arms, and char was etched into the lines crisscrossing her palms. A red weal had bubbled across the pads of her fingers, where hot steel had scorched her skin when she lifted the bolt on the kennel door to free the dogs from the fire.

Sarel twisted her hands behind her.

She didn't want to be reminded of the night before, of the hours she'd spent scrabbling in the dirt, trying to gather enough stones to pile into rocky graves over the still bodies of her parents, of the ash that had drifted down on the evening breeze and filled in the cracks between the stones.

She didn't want to be reminded that her parents had died because of this place. This place that was going to keep Sarel alive whether she wanted it to or not.

MUSA

�֍ �֍ �֍

7

Sivo had never taken him out after dark before. Musa cowered in the back seat of the jeep, watching the sun smear the sky red and gold as it sank between the crumbling buildings. They had been out looking for water every day that week, sweeping farther and farther from the shack in the middle of Tandie territory where they kept Musa.

Where he huddled in the corner, alone, trying not to move so the chains wouldn't cut into his skin. Alone, except when footsteps scuffled in the dirt and a body crouched on the other side of the wall. When he heard breathing, hiccupped and ragged. Sometimes there was even a voice. A voice he knew as well as his own, whispering his name through the rusted gap in the corrugated steel.

Sometimes it was a relief to hear that voice. And sometimes it was a relief to be far away, where the voice couldn't reach him.

Musa rubbed his eyelid, and a crust of dried dirt sifted to the floor. Even the smallest movement sent spikes of pain shooting through his wrists. It was getting worse. Sivo wouldn't give him a single cup of water to clean the sores.

When Musa was little, his mother used to tell stories from when she was a girl, from a time when you only had to turn a handle and water sprayed down on you — hot, cold, and everything in between — just for washing. A time when she and her sisters would run around the neighborhood splashing through the water people sprayed in front of their houses to make the grass turn green.

Musa and his brother, Dingane, had always laughed at that part, sure she was teasing. The idea — people spraying water into the air because they liked green grass instead of brown.

For some reason, when the boys laughed at this, it only made their mother sad.

Musa flinched away from the searing-hot seat buckle that dangled overhead and swung at his bare skin as the jeep rattled down the broken road. He closed his eyes and licked his lips, imagining cool water sprinkling across his face like rain.

The jeep hit a rut and threw him onto the floor. Musa hit the ground face-first, his arms pinned beneath him. The chains at his wrists bit into raw skin, and he cried out in surprise and pain.

Sivo jammed the brakes and jumped out. He leaned over the side of the jeep, his large hands gripping the boy around the ribs and hefting him upright. Sivo took one look at the fresh blood leaking down Musa's hands and cursed.

"Just my luck." He felt for the key ring at his waist and unlocked the chains at Musa's wrists. The metal slid to the floor into a heap like a coiled snake. Sivo jumped into the driver's seat and tossed a rag into the boy's lap. "Don't get your filthy blood all over my seats."

Musa held his wrists over the grimy cloth, watching the blood pool on his skin and slide to the back of his wrists, then fall away.

Why, Dingane? Why?

The engine choked to life and Musa put his arms out to brace himself against the jeep's pitching and rolling. The guard in the passenger seat drummed his fingers against the barrel of the rifle that lay across his lap.

After ten more minutes of bumping and jostling, they pulled over into the shadows a crumbling warehouse cast across a vacant lot. Sivo started to get out of the jeep but the guard shook his head. He spoke for the first time, in a chalky voice. "Not yet. Not until full dark."

Musa settled his hands gingerly in his lap and stretched his legs the length of the back seat. He didn't care why they had stopped, why they were hiding in the shadows like thieves.

He didn't care, until he looked up.

It was the one thing that never changed as they drove from one end of the slums to another. Red scraps of cloth, flags, and ripped T-shirts hung off the corner of roofs, flapping out of windows, and draped over front doors. The mark of Tandie territory.

Musa squinted. Even in the near dark, he could

see that the flag hanging limp from the shattered streetlamp was not red. Cold stole over his skin, down his parched throat, and settled low in his belly.

Musa's breath came short and quick. His mind flooded with memories—a door bursting open, shouting, hands reaching, taking. He squeezed his eyes shut, and a small cry slipped through his lips.

He forced his eyes open again, forced himself to look at the pale cloth, to face what it meant. They had crossed to a part of the city that belonged to another gang.

There was only one reason they would do something so dangerous. The Tandie were out of water.

Musa buried his face in the seat cushions. At least it would all be over soon.

After waiting for half an hour more, Sivo sent Musa out into the empty lot with his dowsing sticks. "Be quick about it," he whispered.

Musa walked out alone, his feet shushing across the dirt. The first stars pricked weakly through the dark sky. Musa lifted his arms and settled into his dowsing shuffle.

The night's silence pressed in all around him. His

heartbeat thundered through his ears and chest and fingertips. Sweat beaded on his upper lip.

A bat keened high above, and seconds later, Musa felt the breath of air from its thin wings raise the hair on his neck. He paced back and forth across the dirt. He was almost to the far end of the abandoned lot when a faint click echoed across the darkness.

He paused, one foot hovering inches above the ground, waiting, listening. For a second, everything was silent.

Crack-crack-crack-crack.

Flashes erupted from behind the warehouse, and heavy footsteps kicked up gravel.

A scream ripped through the night, and an answering volley of gunshots echoed across the vacant lot. Musa jumped. He didn't think. He didn't look back.

He dropped his sticks and ran.

SAREL

❖ ❖ ❖

8

A scattering of rain wet the dust, pinning it to the earth for a little while. Wildflowers sprang up out of the ash, spreading clumps of color along the grotto path. Stubborn desert grasses poked up all over the homestead while Sarel slept in the grotto below, the smell of smoke in her nostrils and gunshots cracking through her dreams.

Days passed under the bald sun, and the new growth withered, sinking into the scorched earth as if it had never risen at all. Only the sunlight peeking around the curved stairs separated day from night for Sarel, who was torn in and out of dreams, waking to find her cheeks wet and her throat ragged.

The dogs left the grotto one by one, licking their jowls and trotting up into the sunlight. She was alone, except for Nandi, who kept watch while she slept. And Ubali, who huddled against the opposite wall, licking his wound clean.

The sound grated against her nerves. It kept her from sleeping. It kept her from slipping into the still, silent place between one breath and the next.

With the sound came the memory: Ubali standing beside her father. Snarling. Lunging. And then the guns.

Ubali had tried to save her father. She should be helping him. Her mother would have known what to do. Sarel traced the pale scar that sliced across the inside of her wrist. It had happened in the city, the last time they had gone.

Her family had piled into the car and driven the potholed highway. They were going to visit friends who had a little boy about Sarel's age. When they arrived, the house was dark, the windows boarded up. Hastily packed boxes filled the living room. There was nowhere to sit.

So they walked to a park nearby, where rusted play structures sprang up out of the weeds and a wrought-iron fence enclosed a sunken pool that had been without water so long a massive crack had split the concrete bowl in half.

While the children played, the adults huddled behind the tire swing, talking in hasty whispers about poisoned groundwater and brackish coastal rivers.

Sarel and the little blond-haired boy slid down the slide over and over again, chased each other around the little park, and climbed onto rubber swings, kicking their legs into the sky and shrieking with laughter.

But then Sarel tripped and fell, the tender skin at her wrist snagging on a scrap of rusted metal.

"She needs a shot and antibiotics," the woman said, her voice climbing high with panic while she clutched her little boy close. "And where do you think she'll get something like that now?"

Sarel's mother mopped up the blood and wrapped a bandage around the cut.

"You see!" the man hissed. "It's not safe here. Not anymore. You should leave too. While you still can."

Sarel's father drove home, his lips drawn in a tight line while he eased the car over bumps and around gaping holes in the highway. But the ride home was Sarel's favorite part of the whole day. Her mother rode in the back seat with her, cradling her in both arms and singing softly over her head.

Sarel never saw the little boy or his parents again. And they never went back to the city.

When the car turned onto the homestead, relief hung in the air like clouds ripe with rain. They were home. They were safe. Sarel's mother clipped bright green spears from the garden, slit them in half, and pressed the gooey underside against the cut, clicking her tongue and smoothing Sarel's sun-bleached hair away from the slicks of tears on her cheeks.

Her mother had always used aloe to soothe a burn or to heal a cut. She had grown the succulents in her garden all year round. When the gourds and climbing beans and sour figs had all bloomed and died back, the aloe stayed. And year after year, as the drought thinned the other plants and cut the crop in half, and then in half again, the aloe remained.

Sarel pushed herself up off the stones. Maybe the aloe had survived the fire. She could get some for Ubali, make him better. Make him stop licking.

Sarel scuffed up the stairs and through the burnt yard, shading her eyes. The air was thick with smoke, and a layer of ash smothered the ground. It hurt to move. It hurt to breathe.

North and east of the homestead, the earth was burned black, straight to the horizon, where a hazy smudge marked the city skyline. To the west stretched bare desert, blurred by undulating waves of hot air. A dry riverbed cut a trench in the dirt to the south, ending abruptly at the base of a low rise encircled by layers of chalky minerals that had leached out of the rocks beneath. The hill was crowned by a copse of sweet thorn trees—the only green things for miles.

Where the house had been, a few black lumps rose out of the char: a cooking stove, the backless frame of a metal chair, a pile of jumbled mattress coils, and a crumbling stack of chimney bricks. At the base of the stove was a lidded jar: a familiar, stout shape. Flour. Sarel's stomach roared.

She waded through the char and hefted the crockery onto her hip. Kneeling in the dirt, she pried open the lid. Like everything else, it was black inside. Sarel closed her lips over a lump of singed flour and ground it between her teeth, tilting her head back to force the paste down her throat. Her eyes watered, and she had to clamp her hand against her mouth to keep from spitting it out again.

The pups padded up to her and whuffled in her face, licking traces of flour from her fingers and thrusting their noses into the jar. The garden. There might be something to eat in the garden. Sarel wavered to her feet and kept walking.

Behind the blackened foundation, a knock-kneed windmill listed in the breeze. The dry well beside it was filled with dust. Beyond the new graves, in the middle of the yard, the kennel stood upright, glinting dully in the sun.

The roof had burned and fallen through the gaps in the chainlink. The dogs panted without any shade, their ribs pumping like bellows. Their tin watering trough was coated with a layer of ash.

The garden lay to the south of the kennel. Sarel's footsteps stuttered as the black ribs of tilled earth came into view. Ruined. Like everything else. The ache in her chest began to burn hot and hard. Tears seeped out of her eyes, cutting trails through the soot that caked her cheeks.

Nandi pressed against her and rubbed the underside of her jaw against the girl's hip. Sarel dropped her hand to worry the soft edges of Nandi's ear between her fingers.

"Nandi." Sarel's voice cracked and she slumped to the ground, holding the dog's face between her palms. Her mouth worked, her breath coming hard and ragged. "What do we do?"

The wild aloe grew out on the flats. She wasn't supposed to go beyond the post-and-rail fence that wound around the homestead without one of her parents by her side. She was too young to be out there alone. But all that was left of the fence was a circle of singed holes in the ground.

This place was her home. And they were her dogs now.

She would have to do this, all of it, alone.

M U S A

❖ ❖ ❖

9

Musa ran through the coal-black night. He tripped over loose stones and discarded scrap metal that littered the clogged city streets, ducking in and out of shadows. He fell again and again, until the skin on his knees and palms was ragged and bloody. He ran for hours over pavement that was buckled and potholed from years of neglect.

Musa's breath scraped through his parched throat—so loud he was sure the sound would give him away and lead the men with their guns right to him. Through any door, behind every tattered window shade, someone could be watching, ready to turn him in. They would hand him over for a single bottle of water.

So Musa ran and didn't look back. The air rattled through his lungs, and his every pulse stabbed at the sores on his ankles and wrists.

When the sky over his shoulder began to pale, the ruined pavement and the press of ramshackle buildings gave way to packed-dirt roads and a few scattered shacks. Musa kept running until he crested a low rise, his feet stuttering at the sudden absence of anything man-made. He stopped, swaying on his feet, and turned to look back the way he had come.

The city filled his vision, the smoggy sunrise bleeding through the gaps between buildings. He squinted, looking for a plume of dust, listening for the sound of an engine revving. But the air was still, and the city, for now, was quiet.

Maybe no one was chasing him. Maybe Sivo had died back there.

Musa turned to face the dusty wasteland that stretched to the horizon: brown dirt, brown grasses, and a few rocky brown hills. Even the trees were brown: leafless skeletons jutting out of the cracked earth.

His body begged for rest, but he couldn't stop. Not yet. Musa limped into the desert.

When the afternoon sun was at its hottest, when he was moments away from collapse, Musa's footsteps led him to the half-buried roots of a baobab tree. He looked up through a tangle of branches casting a web of shade over him.

A thread of song scraped past his throat, lifting into the air and smoothing the pain from his face. Scraps of a lullaby — Dingane's favorite.

I'll find it for you, Umama, Dingane had said each time their mother finished the song. *I'll find the secret of the baobab tree.*

But it was the younger brother who had heard the water stored in caverns inside the massive trunk.

Was that why, Dingane?

Musa laid a hand against the bark.

He could hear it now, a tinny hum tickling the base of his skull. Musa plucked a long, hollow blade of brown grass and worked it into a crease in the bark. He sucked until his cheeks ached, sucked until he thought he would faint. Until water began to trickle onto his tongue.

He drank, his legs wobbling beneath him.

Musa left the straw in place and slung a leg over a low-lying branch. He climbed into the canopy, settled into a wide notch, and sank into sleep.

SAREL

❋ ❋ ❋

10

The aloe grew in the west. Sarel remembered that much from before.

She walked away from the homestead alone. The sky before her was smeared with the grays and butter yellows of dawn. The wind plucked at her tattered cotton shirt and teased the frayed ends of her shorts. Her hands were jammed into fists, her bottom lip caught between her front teeth.

Before she had taken a dozen strides, Nandi loped up to her, tail swinging, nose lifted to catch the scent of the place they were headed. The pups hurried to follow. And then the whole pack was with Sarel, trotting up or falling back, but always surrounding her.

Just like before.

It had been their habit every day, Sarel and her mother, to set out into the desert with a small jug of water, a rifle, and at least five full-grown dogs. Sarel would carry a satchel over her shoulder, the wind lifting it away from her back and cooling the sweaty skin beneath. Coming home, it would bang against the backs of her knees with each step, full of the tough-skinned fruit or tubers they'd gathered.

Every bush and blooming grass was a lesson. Sarel's mother taught her which cacti held water, which grasses made for the tightest weave, what trees had long taproots reaching deep down to hidden pools of water. She learned the secrets of soil and rocks. How limestone, dolomite, and sandstone pulled rainwater down, tunneled it through tiny pores and stored it underground, away from the greedy sun.

Sarel and her mother had always walked away from the city, away from trails others might be wandering. And they never went far. They were out and back every day before the sun was even a quarter of the way across the sky. Her father met them at the gate each time, with a fresh cup of water and a kiss for them both.

They shared the water, drinking it slowly, one sip at a time. In this desert, in this drought, it was good to be careful. No one knew how long the water would last.

Sometimes they found wild onions for dinner; sometimes they brought home a handful of seeds or a shoot wrapped in a damp towel. Always they waited until the sun dragged its heat below the horizon to tuck their treasures into the garden soil and dribble a teaspoon of dishwater over each one.

As Sarel walked, her mother's instructions came back to her, warning her away from burrows and snake holes in the dirt, nudging her toward hollows in the ground where the water might be close enough to the surface to feed the roots of a hardy desert plant.

Without the hoofed animals carving their steps into the hard ground each day, the wind and tumbling weeds had blurred the familiar paths. Sarel and the dogs returned to the homestead that afternoon with nothing but dusty throats and blistered feet. All she wanted was to dip back belowground, to lie on the cool grotto stones and forget about the aloe. Forget about everything.

But the dogs were thirsty. So she shook the soot

out of their drinking trough and wiped it clean with her palm. She pulled a pair of tin buckets out of the charred rubble where the shed had been and banged them together until most of the ash was gone. Sarel stepped onto the well-worn track between the kennel and the grotto, skirting the rocky hummocks that marked her parents' graves.

Tiptoeing down the spiraling stairs, Sarel let the wire bucket handles fall into the crease of her elbow and trailed her fingers along the pebbled walls. Her head dropped belowground, her eyelids fluttering closed as cool air, thick with memory, washed over her skin.

Breathing deep the smell of wet stones, she stepped to the edge of the shallow pool. She lifted a tin ladle off a hook in the wall and dipped it into the water, then filled her buckets slowly. Light flooding down the stairwell bounced against the water and rippled over the mosaic walls.

Her father had made the grotto for her mother. He had dug down into the earth, carving stairs that curved around the edge of a dusty cave, and mortaring stones, bits of pottery, and mirrored shards into the walls. Sarel and her mother and father had come down often to hide from the heat of the day, the sound of their low voices and laughter bouncing against the curved walls.

With the buckets no more than three-quarters full, Sarel scuffed back up the stairs. She glanced around as her head peeked aboveground. But no one was there, just Chakide and Bheka, panting in the heat, ears back and chests heaving.

Sarel's shoulders hunched forward under the weight of the water, and her brow pinched in concentration. Her feet carried her in a slow glide so she wouldn't spill a single drop.

Sarel emptied the buckets into the trough and stepped away through a thicket of wagging tails as the dogs rushed forward to dip their heads in for a long drink.

They licked their wet jowls as they pulled up from the trough, coming to rub a jaw against her ribs or to duck an ear under her fingers. Sarel set down her empty buckets, and the ache under her ribs eased just a little.

She left the dogs under the glaring sun and

slipped back down the curving stairs. She lay on the cool grotto stones and pinned her arms against her ears to muffle the sound of Ubali's licking. Sarel felt the weight of a warm body leaning into the curve of her spine and she turned into it, pressing her face into Nandi's fur.

MUSA

❖ ❖ ❖

II

Musa stayed in the baobab tree for two days, wandering in and out of memory, of nightmare, drinking until the skin no longer hung from his face like that of an old man, until the ripping pains in his belly eased.

Slowly, the memories ordered themselves, his mind sifting through images he had shut out all those weeks in the darkness, when chains shackled him every day to the same filthy corner. Memories of his mother holding him around the waist and splashing a precious cupful of water over his face. Placing dowsing sticks in his hands and lifting his forearms to just the right height, saying, "Steady, now. Listen, my little Musa. Listen."

He remembered running to his brother, Dingane, with the news: "I can hear it! I can hear the water — just like Umama!" And stumbling away, nose gushing with blood, blubbering, bewildered by Dingane's burst of anger.

He saw his mother lying on her bed, her face gray and slick with sweat, her mouth opening and closing again, as if there were something she needed to tell him. He saw the door burst open and burly men in Tandie colors dragging Dingane by the collar into the room, shouting, pointing at Musa. He remembered Dingane's nod, and his wide, panicked eyes. And then the rough hands, grabbing Musa and dragging him out the door, pulling him away from his mother's outstretched arms.

He remembered the voice, Dingane's voice, that whispered through the rusted gap in the corner of the shack. Calling his name. Begging for forgiveness. Whispering that Umama hadn't survived the sickness.

Musa held his ribs as sobs shook through him. His eyes burned and his throat ached, but his body couldn't spare any water for tears.

A moth lifted away from the branch above his

head, twirling upward, leaving silent trails of dust in its wake.

Each day, the water stored inside the tree sank a little lower. Each day, Musa moved the drinking straw closer and closer to the ground. Even the baobab couldn't hold water forever. He couldn't stay there anyway, in the crown of a tree a half-day's walk from the city.

So when the sun lit the sky on his third morning without chains, Musa turned his back to the city, to the bright ball of rising heat.

He took a long, last drink from the baobab tree and began walking.

SAREL

✦ ✦ ✦

12

For the second day in a row, Sarel woke with the first wisps of light and set out to look for the wild aloe. But hours later, her hands empty and her feet sore, she stumbled back onto the homestead. It was harder than she thought it would be, finding the trails they used to walk without her mother to lead the way.

She was tired. And hungry. She wanted to lie down on the cool stones and never get up. But the dogs were panting in the heat of the day, without a roof on the kennel to give them any shade.

Sarel swiped at the sweat dripping into her eyes and squinted up at the hill behind the homestead. The sweet thorn trees perched on top flashed their green leaves and yellow buds at the black earth all around. They looked healthy enough—she could take a strip of bark from each one and weave them through the kennel roof.

At least the winds had blown the fire north and east, away from the little hill and its copse of trees. She would need that bark for medicine and the thorns for needles. And though it wouldn't fill her belly, the sour gum that seeped through cracks in the bark would give her something to chew on.

But she didn't have anything to cut through the bark.

Sarel stumbled over to the sooty remains of the garden shed. The dull edge of a shovel blade poked out of the rubble. She hefted it out of the ashes and set it aside.

Kneeling down, Sarel rooted around in the char, the remains of her mother's gardening tools sifting through her fingers. She brushed against something sharp. A single dot of blood beaded in her palm and she brought it up to her mouth, spitting the ashy blood into the dirt.

Cautiously this time, Sarel reached in and clasped the inlaid-bone handle. It was her father's knife. She wiped the grit away from the blade and cradled the thing between her hands, swallowing around a hard lump in her throat.

Sarel spit into the hinge and worked it back and forth until the knife folded cleanly. She tucked it into her pocket, pressing her hand against its solid weight as she trudged up to the top of the little hill.

Sarel stripped lengths of bark from the sweet thorn trees and tucked them under her arm. She slid down the graveled hillside and crossed the dry riverbed, stepping into a narrow channel that had once diverted water to the garden and kennel, and following it back to the homestead. The pups raced ahead, then dashed back to nip at the bobbing tips of the bark strips.

She paused for a moment to lean against the kennel. She still couldn't take a full breath, not since the fire, not after all that smoke. When her heartbeat settled back into her chest and her breathing slowed, Sarel scaled the wall of the kennel fencing and threaded the bark through the chainlink roof.

The pack watched from below, the pups tilting their heads this way and that, their brows furrowed.

When she was done, the dogs circled, pawed the ground, and lay down in their new rectangle of shade.

Sarel's head throbbed, her mouth dry as a thistle. She climbed down, then stumbled into the grotto and knelt beside the pool of water. She drank, three sips only, holding the last in her mouth until it was as warm as the insides of her cheeks before swallowing.

Finally, she lay down on the stones and clamped her hands against her ears to shut out the sound of Ubali's licking.

NANDI

❖ ❖ ❖

13

Legs stretch long, pups grow into too-big feet.

One impala comes back, leaves scent in dirt, crushes grass for sleeping. Two spring hares duck into burrows, black tails flashing.

Yipping hyena, sharp-teeth jackal follow.

They stay far under sun, come close under moon, sniff-sniff at pack scent. Sharp teeth flash. Yellow eyes blink-blink in dark.

Pups learn scents. Learn to hunt. Learn to stay far from hyena, learn howl of jackal.

Pups stay close under moon.

Scuffle sound, snarl sound. Kennel door clang-clang.

Time for Sarel-girl to come out under moon.

SAREL

❖ ❖ ❖

14

Sarel shaded her eyes with her hand. Something blurred the steady line of the sheltered plain ahead of her. It might only be wisps of heat, or a gust of wind that stirred up the dust. She pattered closer, the earth under her feet cracked and creased as a discarded snakeskin. Brown smudges separated into clumps, individual bushes, rosettes of serrated green spears.

She'd done it. She'd found the bitter aloe.

Sarel dashed forward, relief pulsing through her and prickling the tips of her fingers. The pups romped beside her, heads swinging this way and that to see what had finally lifted the sadness from her slight shoulders.

Sarel sank to the ground beside a large plant with new seedlings spreading in whorls around it. Nandi came to stand beside her, and Sarel threw her arms around the dog's chest, pulling her tight and kissing the backs of her ears.

"We found it!" Sarel whispered, a smile rippling across her lips.

She moved from plant to plant, clipping a spear from each one. Sarel tucked them into her pocket, where the cut ends wept a clear gel that soaked through her thin cotton shorts.

Three spears for Ubali, to draw out the infection. And three for the garden.

When the sun went down, she would prop them upright in the soil. Maybe they would take root; maybe they would grow as large as her mother's plants.

Or maybe nothing would grow in that soil ever again.

They followed a narrow game track homeward, the soles of Sarel's feet lifting a swirl of dust with each step. All around her rippled a flood of tawny, black-mouthed dogs. Sarel held her arms out to her sides and a blunt head nosed under each palm. Her fingers skidded through the slicks of coarse hair running backwards on their spines as the dogs trotted forward, sliding under her hands.

The wind kicked up the top layer of dirt as they walked on to the homestead, and the smell of smoke and char hung in the air. The dogs fanned out as they entered the yard. Bheka and Icibi flopped into side-sprawled naps while the pups wrestled and yipped in the space between them.

Sarel went straight to the grotto. She cut the three spears into squares and pushed Ubali's head out of the way. She pressed the gel against the bullet wound and waited while Ubali relaxed under her hand. He could have thrown her off, but instead, he tucked his head around her leg and began to wash the dirt from her ankles.

Settling to the ground beside Ubali, Sarel looked around the small room. The very stones seemed heavy with sorrow, ringing with the echoes of her screams.

It was time to move out of the grotto. Time to sweep the ash from the kennel floor and stretch out under the stars. She could weave a mat to sleep on and let the warm bodies of her dogs tuck in all around her. It would be safer, anyway, with a latched door between them and the animals that prowled at night. And if the men came back, there would be nothing to lead them to the water, to the arc of stones at the far end of the yard that marked the grotto entrance.

When Sarel made her way aboveground again, the dogs were feeding on the bloody remains of a gazelle. Bheka and Icibi, the proud hunters, lay off to the side, licking their jowls and smoothing the fur on their forelegs.

Sarel eyed the animal. When the pack had all finished, if the hide was in good shape, she would cut it away and dry it like her father had done after a hunt. She would dig out the bladder, careful not to tear the thin membrane, and hang it to dry. And then she would drag the bones away and let the vultures do their work.

Nandi sat primly, waiting for Sarel. Her tail thumped up a cloud of dust, a meaty foreleg dangling from her jaws. Sarel's stomach rumbled and she reached out, taking the food she was offered.

She didn't know how to start a fire to cook it, and the thought of a single lick of flame made her want to retch the few sips of water and grainy tubers she'd eaten that day.

If the dogs didn't need cooked meat, then neither did she.

Sarel hung the meat on a wire to drain the blood and sliced away the hide with her knife.

MUSA

❖ ❖ ❖

15

Musa walked that day as long as he could, walked while the sun rose over his shoulder. Walked while it set, lighting the ground in front of him like a glowing, crimson path.

On the second day, his pace slowed to a limping shuffle. His muscles knotted with cramps while the sun beat the sweat out of him, swelling the air with suffocating heat. But he placed one foot in front of the other, as he had done all day and the day before that.

It became a game, of sorts—to see how long he could ignore the itch between his shoulder blades, how many steps he could take before he had to turn around to be sure the Tandie weren't coming after him.

His shoes fell apart, and he had to shred what canvas was left before wrapping it around the rubber soles and tying them onto his blistered feet. If only he had an extra pair. Or a hat to keep the sun off his head. Or even a blanket to cut the bite of the desert air after the sun set.

They had been ready, once. Ready for the hard journey north, away from the city, away from the gangs and the dead water. Umama had insisted that they wait until they each had packs full of food, canteens, sturdy walking boots, a compass, even a tent.

Dingane had been so proud of that tent. He had worked for weeks on a well crew, the blisters on his palms bubbling and breaking. When he came home with the tent strapped to his back, Umama had tucked it carefully into one of the packs, calling him her big strong boy and kissing him on both cheeks.

"Soon," she had said, her voice pitched low so no one could overhear. "We'll leave this place soon."

But that was before she got sick. Before the fever sank its teeth into her flesh and shook the life from her body.

* * *

Musa slept in the cover of whatever brush or rock pile
he could find, pressing his arms over his ears to shut
out the sounds of the prowling night animals.

On the third day, Musa crossed a dry lakebed littered with stumps and the skeletons of sunken boats.
The clay left behind had broken into a thousand
pieces, turning up at the edges like fallen leaves.

His mind wandered in and out of focus, in and out
of memory, till it seemed that his mother walked with
him.

Listen, my little Musa. Listen.

SAREL

16

Three limp spears of aloe poked out of the soil.

The garden should have been spilling over with life — the horned cucumbers yellowing, the crossberry flowering, the sour figs stretching to fill every corner. Sarel raked her fingers through the lifeless dirt. Shot through with the memory of her mother's hands at work, of her mother's laughter as she plucked a horned cucumber from the vine, bit into the fruit, and wiped a dribble of green juice from her chin, Sarel lay down and pressed her cheek into the charred soil.

She knew the horned cucumbers grew wild in a sandy hollow a half-day's walk to the north and east.

Toward the city. Her eyes flicked from the barren rows of soil to the low angle of the morning sun. Slinging her newly woven satchel over her shoulder, she set off toward the hazy skyline.

Sarel followed a dusty game track, the dogs a steady current eddying around her. They moved through the cool morning until the sun swung overhead and pulled the sweat from her pores. Long, thirsty tongues lolled out of the dogs' mouths.

When the day was at its hottest, the hard line of a highway wavered into view. Sarel paused and Nandi fell into step beside her, grazing against her hip and ducking her head under the girl's hand. Sarel let out a gust of breath. No one traveled the highways anymore. She was still far from the city. Who else would come out here, into the middle of the desert, in the heat of the day?

No one, she told herself. No one.

Sarel crossed the hot asphalt quickly, the mottled surface scalding and foreign under her feet. But she stopped again when they reached the other side. A sheet of colored metal attached to a long pole lay half buried in a crust of grit. Its reflective edges caught the sun's light and threw it into her eyes. Shading the glare with the palm of her hand, Sarel knelt and scraped the words clear.

KARST FLATS

20 KM

Below the lettering, an arrow pointed back the way they'd come. Scrubbing her foot in the dirt, Sarel kicked a layer of dust over the sign. She didn't want anyone going looking for anything in that direction.

The horned cucumber grew just past the highway, in a dip in the ground where the earth had settled lower than everything around it. The woody vine sprawled across the dirt, the fruit tucked away from the harsh sun under limp green leaves. Sarel reached in and yanked out a studded yellow gourd. She opened her knife and sliced the fruit lengthwise. Glistening green seeds spilled out onto her palm and she slurped a gooey mouthful. Her lips puckered at the bitter taste.

Sarel hacked off a few knobby husks that rattled with dried seeds, then picked the rest of the ripening fruit. Chakide and Bheka nosed the dirt beneath her fingers, rooting under her hands to sniff out whatever she was hiding.

Before, Sarel would have laughed. The pups would have licked her face and wiggled their way onto her lap. But that was before.

Instead, she exhaled in a patter of breaths, the lines that creased her brow smoothing for a moment. Nudging their snouts away, Sarel tucked the gourds inside her satchel and turned toward home.

She jogged easily, glad to have the city at her back. Sarel cradled the contents of her satchel, her mind working as her feet shushed across the dirt. The cucumber wasn't the only drought-hardened plant her mother had grown in the garden. And it wasn't the only one that still grew wild.

There was the bitter aloe. And thatches of sweet onion hiding in pockets of shade, and sour figs sprawled wild out on the sandy flats. Maybe she could even grow a mangosteen tree to shade the tilled earth.

As Sarel walked, tufted clouds stretched across the sky, soft and cool as a cotton bed sheet. When they arrived at the homestead, she jogged straight to the garden.

Kneeling down, she brushed away the top layer of fire-blackened earth and raked the soil with her fingers, combing it into neat rows. She pried open the husks and scattered seeds into the shallow channels. She scooped handfuls of dirt to cover them and pressed the ground flat again, the imprints of her fingertips crisscrossing like bird tracks over the buried seeds.

The sun dipped below the horizon as Sarel finished her work. She knew her garden needed water — as a child she had walked often to the river with her mother, hand in hand, and watched as she raised the sluice gate, watched water fill the narrow channel and flood into the planted furrows. But that was before the river went dry.

Sarel's hand closed on empty air. No matter how badly she wanted to see her mother's garden blooming again, she wouldn't use a drop of their drinking water for this. There was no way to know how much longer the old well that fed the grotto pool would have water left to give.

She squinted through the failing light along the half-buried channel to where the sluice gate hung, holding back nothing but air. Sarel knew it wasn't enough, burying a handful of seeds and wishing for rain. But she didn't know what else to do.

She lay down and pressed her cheek into the charred soil.

MUSA

✤ ✤ ✤

17

It wasn't until the fourth day that he felt it—a low hum, like a cloud of buzzing gnats, pulsing through the ground to the west and rising through the soles of his feet to settle at the base of his skull. A hum so slight, it could have been just a headache.

Musa stopped and listened. His body turned toward the sound like a needle on a compass.

Fresh water.

Faint, far away.

But it was there.

SAREL

18

Sarel woke to the wet pattering of drops against her cheek. The air was charged with a musky, moist smell. She lay still for a moment, her mind blinking into focus. Nandi was up, her nose pressed through a gap in the chainlink fencing, a high-pitched whine rising from her throat.

Sarel jumped up, a word forming on her lips.

Rain.

She dashed to the gate, lifted the bolt, and sprinted outside. Above, tearing winds whipped dark clouds across the sky. The dogs burst into the yard, lunging and swatting at each other, rolling in the wet dust, lifting their snouts to the air and barking at the rain as it fell.

Sarel ran back inside and dragged the trough to the front of the kennel, where a steady line of water dripped from the edge of the roof. She grabbed her buckets and placed them at the corners. Hurrying inside again, she untied the two bladders she had saved, catching them as they fell from the roof and re-tying them under channels of rainwater.

The dogs stopped their play and sat in a tidy row around the edge of the kennel, licking the drips that coursed down the steel bars. For once, their tails thumped the dirt without lifting a cloud of dust. Sarel gripped the chainlink and pulled herself up to catch a stream of gritty, metallic raindrops in her upturned mouth.

Mirrored in the drops of water running down the fence, a white flash split the sky behind her. Lightning.

The chorus of insects that had risen to greet the rain fell silent.

"No," she whispered, whipping around, her eyes scanning the desert for smoke. "No, no, no."

A low rumble of thunder moved through the earth and Nandi came to stand beside her. Sarel buried her hand in the fur at Nandi's neck and gripped tight.

Flashes of light danced through the clouds, but none struck the ground. No sheets of fire raced through the grass toward the homestead.

The storm blew past.

Breaking through the clouds, the sun sucked the moisture out of the air. The dogs wandered from puddle to puddle, noses in the dirt, licking up bits of pooled water. As the last few drops slid between cracks in the ground and disappeared from sight, the dirt paled as if it had never even rained.

Sarel tore her gaze away from the storm clouds. Her grip loosened and she smoothed the damp fur at Nandi's neck. It was always the same once a storm passed. Fear drained from her blood, leaving prickling relief. Relief—but regret, too. Regret that the clouds were gone, that they hadn't let loose their full weight of water.

Sarel peered over her shoulder at her garden. A small smile twitched at the corners of her mouth.

It had rained, and maybe it would even be enough.

MUSA

19

Musa stumbled and fell. He rolled onto his back, arms falling limp at his sides.

Even with his eyes closed, the sun burned into him, round black spheres boring into the backs of his eyelids. His skin was caked with filth, and the sores at his wrists and ankles had begun to fester, shooting burning pain up his arms and legs.

The air was dead.

The wind filled his mouth with ashes.

Up. He had to get up now, or he never would. Musa rolled over. He scrabbled to his hands and knees and pushed himself upright.

He was close. He could feel it.

Spots floated across his vision and Musa lifted a hand to shade his eyes. He looked west. The earth was a brown blur straight to the horizon. It was mad, searching for water in the driest corner of the desert. But then, who would bother to look for him there?

Maybe the Tandie would just let him be.

SAREL

❖ ❖ ❖

20

Sarel squatted by the edge of the grotto pool, arms wrapped around her shins and her chin perched on her knees. She traced the chalky water lines that started at the tips of her toes and circled downward like rings marking a tree's years.

She dipped a finger into the pool. It touched bottom before the water reached her wrist.

Sarel lurched to her feet, crossing to the pump handle. Even though she had already tried a dozen times, she yanked the ribbed steel down and back up again, grunting with the effort. Down and up, down and up, like a needle stitching without thread.

The well was dry.

They had been so careful. For years, so careful with every single drop. But none of that mattered. It was all gone.

Sarel scooped a palmful of water into her mouth and rolled it around inside her cheeks and under her tongue before letting it slide slowly down her throat. She filled one bucket half full and walked up the curving stairs. Each slow footfall scraped against the stone steps as she made her way aboveground.

She crossed the yard, not looking at the slab of cement where her home had been, or at her parents' bare graves, not looking to where cucumber shoots, thin as blades of grass, peeked out of the garden soil.

What did that matter if they had to leave this place? Beside the path, a beetle burrowed into the ground, its hind legs skittering against the hard earth.

Sarel emptied her bucket into the trough. The dogs came running at the sound of the water splashing against the tin walls. She waded between their sinuous bodies, tails thwacking her shins and calves as she passed.

Collapsing onto her woven grass bed, Sarel blinked back the stinging in her eyes and counted the water skins hanging from the ceiling like slumbering bats. There were two that needed stitching and sealing before they could hold water. In the morning, she would fill the rest. That might last the pack a few days.

They had to go. But the thought of leaving this place made the air burn in her lungs, as if she were still drinking down smoke with every breath.

Her mother had taught her to read the landscape, to look for hollows and shadows that might hide the next day's meal. Sarel had to believe that if she looked hard enough, she would find water somewhere out in the desert. Somewhere they hadn't looked yet. Plants with taproots like the sweet thorn trees could find water anywhere. Or she could follow the tracks of the grazing animals. Anything still alive out there was getting water somehow.

Sarel rose to her feet. There was enough daylight left for her to gather a few needles and begin stitching. Pushing her hair out of her face and wiping her eyes with the back of her hand, she walked toward the dry riverbed. The dogs followed her, sniffing at the dust-clogged bedrock and running up, then leaping off the cut bank.

As they neared the low rise, the height of the

riverbanks on either side fell, until at last, at the base of the hill, the ground leveled off completely. The sweet thorn trees at the top cast long shadows in the dimming light.

On top of the hill, the dogs trotted beyond the reach of the branches, well clear of the divots that riddled the ground and the long thorns that gave the trees their name. Every time Sarel came up here, the ground seemed rougher, the divots sinking deeper, exposing more of the trees' dark roots. She placed her feet carefully, stooping to pick a dozen thorns out of the dirt. The small ones made the best needles, and she always split a few thorns down the middle before she notched a clean eye.

Sarel looked out through the curtain of green leaves that surrounded her. Beyond the trees, a raptor circled on the cooling currents of air, its mournful cry lapping against the barren earth. Maybe she should have started her garden up here, where growing green things didn't seem to mind the drought.

Not that it would have mattered. She couldn't keep her dogs alive on fruit. They needed water. Sarel turned in a slow circle. She squinted, tried to see as far as she could—looking in the distance for a glimmer of anything wet, anything green.

Which way should they go?

Not toward the city. Not toward the coast, where the rising sea made everything it touched undrinkable. Not south, where nothing lived, where even the animals wouldn't go.

West, then.

Sarel moved from tree to tree, slicing off strips of gum that seeped out of the bark. When she had two handfuls, she stuck a piece in her mouth, chewing as she plodded downhill.

They would leave in the morning.

She called the dogs to the kennel for the night. Nandi swiveled an ear back at the sound of her name, but she didn't come. Sarel walked to where the dog sat, staring east into the growing dark. She rubbed a hand over Nandi's blunt head and tugged gently at her ruff.

Nandi followed, but she paused every few steps to look back over her shoulder.

NANDI

21

Sarel-girl says, "Come." Makes pile of water skins. "Nandi, come!"

I turn away. I sit, eyes watching sun-up side.

I do not come.

Icibi, Thando sit, heads swing side-side. Sarel-girl says, "Come," command of Man-with-whistle.

I say no.

Pups make low whine, uneasy whine.

Sarel-girl flaps arms. Returns water skins to kennel. Sits on ground. Puffs air through nose.

Not anger scent from Sarel-girl. Fear scent. Worry scent.

Buttu bumps water skins with snout. Licks nose.

Licks empty trough. Thirsty whine. Buttu lies with Sarel-girl, head on lap. Thirsty whine.

I lift nose, sniff-sniff.

Boy coming soon.

Boy with the water song inside.

Sarel-girl rubs snout of Buttu. Gets up, empties water skin to trough. Pups jump up, old dogs run like pups, slurp-slurp. All drink.

Water gone.

Sarel-girl looks at empty skin, thirsty dogs, throws skin to dirt.

Rustle sound from unwele bush.

Ears prick. Pack all stand and point, hackles up.

Boy steps from bush, stumble-walks. Sun on dark skin, glint-glint.

I stay, tail down, no fear. Chakide, Bheka lie down, ears up. Eyes to me, eyes to boy. Eyes to me, eyes to boy. I lick paw slow, no anger, no fear. Thando, Icibi, Ubali lie down.

Slap-slap-slap. Sarel-girl sees boy, runs to me, eyes, scent, all, fear-fear-FEAR. Shakes like isundu leaf. Points finger, yells, "Attack! Nandi—attack!"

Buttu jumps up, snarls, tail up.

I show teeth.

Buttu lies down, belly to dirt. Bheka whines. Eyes to me, eyes to girl. Eyes to me, eyes to boy.

"Nandi," Sarel-girl whines like pup.

Boy stumble-walks close. Sour scent, blood scent. Legs thin, wobble like onogola bird.

I stand, walk to Sarel-girl. Look into her fear-fear-FEAR. Walk to boy. Sniff blood at hands, blood at feet. Circle. I stand in front of boy, show to pack.

Bird-legs-boy with water song has come.

SAREL

22

Sarel balled her fists, the breath stuck in her lungs. Nandi stood in front of the boy, the coarse hair on her back nearly reaching his ribs. Sarel knew that stance, the protective set of Nandi's shoulders.

The boy just stood there, arms hanging limp at his sides. Wide brown eyes darted around the pack of dogs that surrounded Sarel. His skin showed through caked dirt like fissures in the earth. He said something—something about water. And then he swayed and crumpled to the ground in a puff of dirt.

Sarel stared at the heap of skin stretched over too-thin bones. She knew that sound—the sound a body made collapsing in a heap, the dust settling over it, the life slipping away from it. She knew the silence that followed.

Nandi stood over the boy. She sniffed his face and licked his sores, first at the wrists and then the ankles. She circled the body once, her tail swinging low.

"Nandi," Sarel pleaded.

Nandi settled onto her haunches beside the boy, lowering her chest slowly to the ground. She watched Sarel under heavy lids.

Sarel spun on her heel, kicking the pebbles out of the path on her way to the kennel. Chakide followed behind her, nipping at her heels and chasing down the bouncing pebbles, only to spit them out again, lick and sneeze the dust off his muzzle. Sarel pulled out her knife and sliced down the center of her sleeping mat. She stared, hands on hips, at the two mats lying side by side on the dirt.

Sarel tucked a toe under the boy's half and kicked it to the opposite corner of the kennel.

Stalking over to where the boy lay, she grabbed him under his arms and stumbled backwards, his heels drawing twin lines in the dirt. The skin over the boy's ribs pulled tight and his shorts slid down, revealing sharp hipbones that jutted out to each side. Sarel squatted down and rolled him off her, wrinkling her nose at the stench.

She lurched to her feet, her eyes roving from the boy's festering sores to his bony elbows and knees. His lips were cracked and bleeding, and his eyelids hung slack, the whites of his eyes yellowed and tacky. His pulse raced beneath paper-thin skin and his legs twitched as if he were still stumbling across the desert.

What was he running from?

The sores on his wrists and ankles looked like the marks a collar might leave, if it was bound too tight. Sarel's father had told her of people who collared their dogs, chaining them to one place so long that sores sprung up on the skin.

Who would do that to a little boy? A shiver rippled across her shoulders.

Who was he running from?

The dogs swiveled, all at once, ears pricked, eyes fixed on a jumble of rocks just past the homestead. A chittering alarm sounded, and the small hairs at the back of Sarel's neck stood on end. Seconds later, a dark blur dove out of the clouds. The raptor screamed, then banked away from the rocks, a wriggling dassie rat trapped between its claws.

Sarel's hands were still clenched as she turned back to the boy lying at her feet. "I don't know why you want to keep him."

Nandi ducked her head under Sarel's fingers, twisting her neck to look up into the girl's face.

Sarel felt the resistance leave her body in a long breath. The boy would need water, and food. Not that they had any to spare.

Sarel opened her woven grass satchel and frowned at the clump of fruit and aloe she had gathered that morning. Food that she had planned to take with her when they left the homestead for good. She spilled it all onto her mat and began cutting the aloe spears into short, juicy strips.

Fine. She would get the boy healthy.

But then he was on his own.

MUSA

✦ ✦ ✦

23

Light lay across Musa's face in uneven stripes. He could feel it warm on his cheeks and glowing orange against the insides of his eyelids. He lay on his back, on something almost soft, his legs and arms splayed at all angles.

He blinked. There wasn't ever any light in his shack, and Sivo never let him just lie around without his hands and feet chained.

Musa blinked again and rolled his head to the side. His breath caught in his throat with a rasping sound and he coughed, his whole body seizing.

Lying nose to nose with him was the largest dog Musa had ever seen. She had a black snout and soft

wrinkles puckering the space between rich, brown eyes. Her coat was cinnamon-colored, lying like a thick blanket over hard muscles. The hair ran backwards along her spine, all the way up to her neck.

The dog whipped her tail through the air, and a pink tongue shot out and licked Musa on the nose. He jerked back, his hands flying up to protect his face. The air filled with dust from the dog's thumping tail, and Musa sneezed.

He lifted his hands away from his face and stared at his wrists in surprise. Strips of a green plant with a tough outer skin and a gooey underside were wrapped around them. He lifted a wobbling leg into the air and turned it from side to side. His ankles, too.

Sivo had never bothered to heal the boy's cuts and sores—as long as Musa could stand and shuffle around with his dowsing sticks, little things like wrists worn raw didn't matter.

Musa lowered his leg. He propped himself up on his elbows and looked around. He was in a large wire cage; there was nothing but dry desert grasses, withered shrubs, and hard dirt beyond. Someone had woven bark through the steel links in the roof, enough to shade a trough for the dogs, the mat he lay on, and

another bed of sorts tucked into the opposite corner. A rock held open the chainlink door.

Musa sank down onto the mat. His arms ached from holding himself up, even for such a short time. The dog crept closer, sniffing at his breath and nudging his fingers.

The door was open. No one was guarding him, except maybe the dog. But she didn't seem to want to hurt him. He could leave. He wasn't a prisoner here.

Movement outside the kennel caught Musa's attention. A girl with white-blond hair cut in a jagged line at her chin strode through the yard, a dozen dogs trotting around her. Ruddy skin peeked out of patchwork clothes that hung from her like laundry on a line. She was thin, but she didn't look weak. Her head swiveled toward Musa, her pale eyes narrowing. Her whole body stiffened and her hands curled into the fur of the dog at her hip.

The Tandie had said that no one could survive outside the city. But there she was, frowning over Musa, her gaze moving from the dog at his side and back to him again. She shrugged a bulging satchel over her head, knelt beside him, and upended a scattering of fruit onto the ground. Her mouth pulled in a tight line as she sliced through the rind of a thin-skinned mangosteen and pried the halves apart.

Musa swallowed, saliva trickling into his mouth as he watched her lick a drop of juice off her palm.

"Why are you helping me?"

The girl flinched at the sound of his voice. She arranged the fruit on a leaf and slid it over to him, shifting to unwrap the vines that held the aloe in place around his ankles.

Musa looked away from the angry, glistening flesh underneath.

"Who are you?"

Her hands stilled. She didn't look up when she spoke.

"Sarel." She formed the word thickly, as if it were unfamiliar on her tongue. "Eat."

Musa picked up a mangosteen and placed it in his mouth. He chewed and tried to swallow, but his throat was too dry and instead he sputtered, choking. Sarel exhaled in a sharp burst and pulled him upright until he was hunched over, spitting the seed into his palm. The dog was on her feet now, nosing her blunt head under Musa's chin and licking the juice from his jaw.

Musa stared at the massive head in front of him. "I've never seen a dog friendly like this—somebody's pet. In the city, dogs are wild. They're mean."

"It's people that make dogs mean," Sarel said in a clipped voice. "And they're not my pets."

Musa tried another bite. He swallowed, this time without choking.

Sarel tied off the vines that held the fresh bits of aloe in place around his ankles and moved up to his wrists. She peeled back the yellowed strips one by one.

Musa didn't ask any more questions. As soon as Sarel finished the last knot, she backed away from him. She slung the empty satchel over her shoulder and hurried out of the kennel, as if she couldn't get away from him fast enough.

The dogs shook as they stood, whipping a spray of dust into the air and trotting after her. Sarel hadn't gone a dozen steps when the big one with the watching eyes rubbed up against her, shoving her snout under the girl's hand. The tension in Sarel's shoulders slackened and her body settled into a shuffling rhythm as they set out again into the desert.

Musa rolled onto his side and folded his knees into his chest. She was the one acting like a mean city dog—scared and bone-thin and ready to bite. So why was she helping him?

It didn't matter. He had made it. He could feel the water, a constant thrum at the base of his skull. Underground, just south of where he lay, wide around as a lake.

In the morning, when he was feeling stronger, Musa would find a new pair of dowsing sticks and mark out the edges—see if he could find a place where the water came aboveground.

If it ever did.

But he couldn't let *her* see. If Sarel found out what he could do, she might betray him, like Dingane. Or use him. Hurt him, like Sivo.

No, he wouldn't tell her anything. He would have to find the water without her watching. No one would have that kind of power over him again.

SAREL

✦ ✦ ✦

24

Everything Sarel owned was spread out on the mat in front of her. A bone-handled knife, a square of leather pierced with a dozen sweet thorn needles, a long-stemmed ladle, and a blunt shovel blade with a branch lashed to the place where a handle should have been.

Three deflated water bladders were stacked in her lap. Sarel nodded as she counted, her forehead pinched in concentration. Six more lined the fence, belled out with all the water she could scrape from the grotto pool. There was enough left in the gaps between stones to last the pack the few days more she'd need to find fruit and nuts to equal the water. It took twice as long, gathering food for Musa, too. But she was almost ready.

She rolled up to her feet and paced the length of the kennel, stepping over the sprawled dogs in her way. Musa was sleeping in the corner, an arm draped over Chakide's ribs. They had to go, whether he had recovered enough to travel or not. Sarel swatted through a cloud of gnats, slapping at the air long after the swarm had gone.

Back and forth she paced, back and forth.

And then she stopped and swiveled, peering across the homestead to the curve of stones that marked the grotto entrance.

They had to go. But she would take something from this place with her.

Sarel swiped the knife off her mat and shuffled down the grotto path. She checked over her shoulder, to make sure no one was watching, and ducked down the curving stairs. Her eyes went straight to the spout and the ring of burnished stones that surrounded it.

Sarel unfolded her knife and dug at the mortar around a white stone with a black vein through its center. She worked carefully, leaning into the mosaic wall and squinting in the dim light.

With a *click* that echoed through the small room, the stone dropped from the wall into Sarel's palm. Her fingers curled around its smooth edges and gripped tight.

MUSA

25

The pack returned, tails high, prancing around Icibi and Buttu and Thando, who dragged a bloodied wildebeest between them. Musa watched the dogs, their muscles bulging, drag the animal across the dirt. Weakened by hunger and dehydrated as it was, their kill was still three times the size of the biggest dog.

Nandi rose and sniffed the carcass. The other dogs waited, licking their jowls, tails sweeping up a cloud of dust. Nandi sank her teeth into the tough hide, the muscles of her hind legs straining against the ground as she pulled. She ripped off a leg and brought it to Sarel, who took the offering and began stripping away the hide, draping lengths of flesh and sinew over the links in the fence.

Musa winced at the dripping blood. "Aren't you going to cook that?"

Sarel ignored him.

"Won't we get sick?"

"Do I look sick to you?" she snapped.

Musa didn't answer. Instead, he began collecting sticks and bits of dried grass and tucking them under his arm. Like a chicken pecking at feed, he bent and righted himself again, making a slow loop around the homestead.

When he returned and dropped his pile of sticks, Musa scraped away a bare patch of earth downwind from the kennel. He paused for a minute, leaning against the steel post, waiting for his breath to slow.

Next he set out for rocks, his whole body leaning back to offset their weight as he carried one at a time and arranged them in a tight circle. Then he turned his back to the wind, dropped a tuft of brown grass into the center of the ring of stones, and hunched low to the ground, rubbing a pair of sticks together until a thread of smoke rose into the air.

Each day, while Sarel was out foraging for food, he had walked to the dry riverbed, to the edge of the water. His limbs trembling with the effort, he had stood above the vast underground lake, the strength of it humming through him.

Musa had seen the scorched rectangle where a house had been and the pair of rocky graves in the middle of the yard. He had seen enough to know why Sarel turned away from the fire, cringing as if the dry crackle of twigs grated against her eardrums. To understand why she crouched, ready to break into a run at any moment.

Musa fed the tiny flame that burst from the tinder until it crackled into a small fire. He speared the strips of meat and dangled them over the flame. The juices popped and sizzled as they fell onto the coals. His stomach gurgled as the oily scent rose into the air, his mouth filling with saliva.

When a pocket of sap burst, loud as the crack of a gun and scattering a spray of sparks across the dirt, Sarel shot up into the air.

Musa ducked his eyes away from the terror that washed across her face. He shifted until his back was to her, until his thin frame blocked the dancing flames from her view. He waited until the meat had cooled and he had stamped out the last of the coals before he brought Sarel her share.

She took it and she ate. But it was late, the stars high overhead, before the tremors coursing through her thin frame finally stopped.

SAREL

✤ ✤ ✤

26

Sarel picked her way along the path to the kennel, and the dogs padded quietly behind her. It had been a long day, but her satchel was full of aloe spears and wild pears and sour figs.

It didn't matter where she walked — the earth was parched, dotted with a few hardy plants that somehow sucked enough moisture out of the ground to stay alive. Even those few were smaller and shriveled and harder to find.

With a long sigh, Sarel closed the chainlink door behind her, latching the pack inside for the night. Musa's eyes flew open as the U-shaped bolt clanged shut, and he flung his hands up to shield his face.

Sarel lowered her eyes while his breathing settled back to normal, squeezing herself between Nandi and Buttu, who were turning in tight circles over her sleeping mat. She rolled onto her back and tucked her arms under her head as the dogs flopped on either side of her.

Dusk bled into dark, broken only by the lonely call of a banded owl.

Sarel woke suddenly in the middle of the night, her hair matted with sweat, her cheeks wet. She gasped for breath, blinking back the memory of guns and blood and suffocating smoke.

She reached for Nandi, but the dog wasn't there.

Sarel propped herself up on her elbows and looked around. It was quiet, except for a thin scraping sound to the south. The full moon shone out of a clear, cold sky. White light glinted off the chainlink fencing and the moist tips of the dogs' noses, off the chalky white deposits that marked the steep hillsides in the distance and the flickering leaves of the sweet thorn trees that danced on snatches of wind. The open kennel door swung inward, clanging like a bell as it struck against the steel post and swung out again.

The door was open.

Sarel's eyes flicked to Musa's mat. The boy was gone.

Despite the chill in the night air, Sarel felt her face begin to pulse with heat. Her breath came fast and ragged, and she stormed out of the kennel, eyes scanning the homestead for any sign of him.

On the bank of the dry river, Nandi sat erect, in the elegant posture Sarel's father had demanded of all his dogs. Nandi turned her head to watch Sarel's approach. The pups sprawled around their mother, only interested in using the night for sleeping, no matter where they lay. Every few seconds, Musa's head appeared then ducked below the cut bank again as he lifted and scattered shovelfuls of dirt.

"What are you doing?" Sarel shouted.

Musa spun around, twisting the shovel behind his back, his free hand falling open.

"You sneak out in the middle of the night, take the dogs, and leave the kennel door unlatched—to do what, dig a hole in the dirt?"

"I—I was just . . ." Musa bit his lip. He kicked the walls of the shallow hole he had dug. "I thought if

I found water, it would help all of us. I wanted to help. I would have died if you didn't help me."

Sarel ignored the pleading note in his voice. "And what makes you think you could dig a hole in the desert and hit water?"

Musa mumbled into his chest, "I thought, if the river was here once . . ."

Sarel's feet were planted wide in the dirt, her stick-straight arms ending in balled fists. "I don't care what Nandi wants. I don't trust you!"

Musa glared back, his nostrils flaring with short, angry breaths. He threw the shovel down into the dirt, scrambled up the bank, and ran to the kennel.

Sarel watched him go. The dogs twined all around her, rubbing the goose bumps from her arms and licking her fists until they unclenched. Nandi came to stand in front of Sarel, her nose inches from the girl's chin. Sarel lifted a hand to worry the wrinkles between the dog's eyes, Nandi's calm gaze smoothing the raw edges of her anger.

Sarel roused the pups, and they walked back to the kennel. She lowered the bolt and crossed to her mat. Icibi and Thando stood, shook off the dust that had settled on their coats, and wedged themselves behind her knees and under her ribs, surrounding her on all sides like a warm, breathing blanket.

Nandi lay in the space between the boy and girl, her ears pricked. She lifted her head, looking from one to the other, and then staring out into the darkness beyond the kennel.

There was a scuffle, a yowl, and a piercing, short-lived scream. And then everything was quiet.

MUSA

❖ ❖ ❖

27

Musa held a tangle of dry grass in his hands. His legs were crossed beneath him and beginning to tingle. But he couldn't move. Sarel had told him to sit there, to try weaving a satchel of his own. He was sure that if he shifted his weight even a little, the whole mess would fall apart in his hands.

In the opposite corner of the kennel, Sarel was counting and separating the water bladders. They were lined up in three little clumps.

Three days of water. If they were careful.

"We're leaving." Sarel didn't look at him as she spoke. "Tomorrow."

"But why?"

"Why? We can't just sit here and do nothing. The water is gone."

But it wasn't. He just hadn't found where it came to the surface yet. "Where will you go?"

"West."

No. That was wrong. There was no water to the west. It was south, just beyond the dry river.

Nandi lifted her head where it had been resting between the two of them, yawned with a long flick of her tongue, and nudged her nose under the boy's hand. Musa stroked the hollows behind her ears.

He had to tell Sarel. He couldn't let her leave, let her take the dogs into the desert to die. Musa's tongue worked in his mouth, worked around the fear that clamped his throat closed.

He had to tell her.

"You learned about dogs from your father, right?"

Sarel's eyes narrowed. "What does that have to do with anything?"

"I learned dowsing from my mother." Musa's eyes flicked up, searching her face. "Anybody can do it—walk around with a pair of sticks, let them show you where the water is. Most people just don't know how."

Musa blew a gust of air to cool the sweat beaded on his upper lip and trickling down his temples. "But there's more to it. You know how you can smell rain in the air before it falls? Or how a thunderstorm lifts the hair on your arms? It's the same with water. You just have to know what it feels like, what to listen for."

"You're telling me you can hear water. Water that's under the ground?"

Musa's bony shoulders bobbed up and down in a quick shrug. "It's how I came to this place."

"Well, you came here for nothing, then. There's no water here. Not anymore. Besides, you're not the only one who knows things. I don't need any sticks to tell me that you look for water where plants are still growing in the middle of a drought."

Sarel flung her arm upward, toward the hill across the dry river. "If there was any water here, it would be there. Those sweet thorn trees are the only green things for miles. What—does water run uphill for you too? Or will you try to dig down as deep as their taproots reach?" She shook her head. "Impossible."

Musa looked out at the desert beyond the riverbed. "I could show you if I had my sticks."

"It will take more than a couple of stupid sticks to—"

"It's here," Musa interrupted. "I know it is."

"Then why haven't I seen it? I've been all over this desert. There is nothing out there. Nothing but dust."

"It could be really deep. Water under the ground takes the same shapes as it does above ground—lakes, rivers, even waterfalls. But if we follow the edges of the water, we might find a place where it comes up to the surface." Musa twisted the mess in his hands, struggling to bend the fibers into place. "I just can't tell how far down it is. I never learned that part."

Sarel crossed the space between them, nudging splayed legs and tails out of the way. She straightened the weave under Musa's fingers, yanking the brittle grasses tight as she spoke. "That doesn't make any sense. If anything, the land south of here is even drier. We'll use every last bit of water we have wandering around, looking for something that isn't there."

"But it is. I know it. You'll see—the sticks cross when they pass over water."

Sarel smoothed the space between Chakide's ears and dusted her hands off on her ragged patches of clothing. "I don't believe you." Her eyes snagged on the puckered pink flesh at Musa's wrists and ankles.

Musa ducked his head under her gaze. He knew why she was staring. He knew what she wanted to know.

"When I was little, and the sea ate up the coasts, the city flooded with people. There wasn't enough food or water for everyone. Anyone with money to buy a way out was gone.

"People said the drought would end, that things would get better. But it didn't. The gangs took over, and they hacked the city into pieces. They took the petrol, so no one could leave. They said they needed it to look for water in the desert, for all of us. But they never found any. And then they just started killing each other and anyone who kept their water to themselves, or tried to survive on their own."

Musa paused, looking out at the graves and the blackened foundation.

"But you know about that."

Silence stretched between them like the wide-flung branches of an umbrella tree. Musa's hands began to work again at the weave in his lap.

"We were going to leave. We had a plan, but my

mother got sick. My brother, Dingane, told one of the gangs what I could do."

Musa's hands fell slack, the brittle grasses slipping out of the weave. "I don't know why he did that."

"And your mother?"

Musa swallowed. "I never saw her again."

Chakide laid his head on Musa's thigh.

"The Tandie locked me up, and only let me out to look for water. But it didn't do any good. The ground-water up there — it's all gone bad."

"But you escaped . . ."

The words were barely out of Sarel's mouth when she lurched to her feet, pacing the length of the kennel and back again. Her fist closed over something small and white.

"What if this gang follows you out here?"

Musa rubbed the new skin at his wrists. He didn't know what to tell her.

What he did know, what he had decided in the long days traveling across the desert to get here, was that he would rather die than be caught by the Tandie again.

SAREL

❖ ❖ ❖

28

Sarel dumped an armful of branches on the ground at Musa's feet.

"Show me."

Musa picked through the pile. He chose an evenly weighted pair, snapping them a hand's-breadth past the forks, trimming and peeling the branches until they swung cleanly in his hands.

"Thank you," he said solemnly. When Musa curled his fingers around the forked ends, his eyelids fluttered closed, as if relieved to feel their weight in his hands.

"You'd better be right about this." Sarel tossed the rest to the dogs. They snapped and lunged at one another, growling playfully and prancing ahead, the sticks clamped between their teeth.

They crossed the dry river and Sarel stopped, hands on her hips, waiting. Musa lifted his arms until the sticks jutted out in front of him. He shuffled forward. After a dozen paces, the sticks swung inward, crossing each other and slapping against Musa's chest. He bent and scratched a line in the ground. Then he backed up and over a few paces, starting forward again.

Sarel rolled the smooth white stone around in her palm as she watched Musa's halting progress. The pups watched too, ears cocked, their eyes following the bobbing tips of the sticks, sure it was a game meant for them.

The scratch marks curved toward the hill until Musa's toes scrabbled against the steep rise.

"That's the edge of the water—those scratches?" Sarel asked.

Musa turned, nodding, and stumbled toward her. "Water comes up to the surface at the edges," he said. The sticks swung away until they slapped the sides of his arms, pointing back to the hill behind him as Musa stepped toward her. "So we—"

"Wait," Sarel interrupted, holding up a hand and pointing. "Why did they do that?"

Musa peered over his shoulder at the sticks angled back behind him. His hands fell to his sides and he dug the tips of the dowsing sticks into the ground.

"I don't know."

This was ridiculous. All of it.

Sarel watched frustration ripple through him. Musa wanted her to believe him. Badly. Why? Sarel ticked her head to the side, considering. What if he was telling the truth? What if she didn't have to leave this place after all?

"The wind will sweep away your scratches before the morning is over. If this is going to work, we have to mark your lines with rocks or something."

Musa's eyes grew wide, and his lips twitched upward.

"I'm not saying I believe you." She toed a trench in the dirt. "It's just . . . Is it big? — the water. Is there enough for all of us?"

"More than enough. If we can get to it."

A gust of wind lifted the dust at her feet and spun it around her ankles.

"If we're not going too far from here, then we

can come back at night. We can sleep in the kennel. It would be safer."

Sarel felt Nandi's eyes on her. The dog sat beside Musa, watching Sarel, waiting.

"But you've already decided, haven't you?"

Nandi stood. She crossed the space between them and placed her chin in Sarel's outstretched hands.

"All right, girl. We'll do it your way."

SAREL

❖ ❖ ❖

29

Sarel settled a water skin into her satchel beside a clump of aloe and a few wrinkled sour figs, and another into the satchel she had woven for Musa. She pocketed her knife and tucked the ladle into her waistband, hefting the shovel like an oversize walking stick.

The homestead was quiet when they left, except for the old windmill, creaking in the early morning breeze. While Musa followed the twitching dance of the dowsing sticks, Sarel kept her eyes on the ground, looking for divots in the earth or bedrock or a cluster of stones that might hide a small spring. Every dozen paces, she scooted a rock to mark Musa's lines in the dirt.

They followed the edge of the water over bluffs dotted with withered scrubs and through dusty flatlands, sometimes following well-worn game tracks, other times picking their way across ground touched only by the scouring winds.

They stopped at midday and rested in the shade of a quiver tree. Ubali rolled over Sarel's outstretched legs, belly up, begging to be scratched. Chakide sat beside Musa's slumped form and licked the sweat and dirt from his face.

Sarel's foraging trips had kept her muscles limber and strong, thin as she was. But Musa still hadn't recovered. He was tired and jumpy, always looking over his shoulder and starting at odd sounds.

They rested for an hour before Sarel called them back to their feet. Musa stood when she stood, and he kicked his legs and leaned side to side, stretching, mimicking her every move.

Sarel went from dog to dog, holding the ladle under their chins for a drink. Tawny tails thumped the ground as she approached, and long pink tongues licked wet jowls as she moved on. Then she tipped the water bladder back, holding it steady as a thin stream of water trickled into Musa's mouth. Finally, she took a few sips herself, swirling the water around in her mouth and letting it slide slowly down her throat.

"Nandi," she said when the empty water bladder was stowed back in her satchel, "let's go home."

Nandi lifted her nose and set out across the desert. The pack followed, tails hanging a little lower than they had that morning.

NANDI

❖ ❖ ❖

30

I leave my kennel. Leave place with fire scent in air, fire dust in ground.

Days are long. Paws crack, bleed. Dust in nose, dust in eyes, dust in air.

Ground is thirsty, trees thirsty, pups thirsty. Make low whines, thirsty whines. Panting, panting.

I pass bones in dirt, bones with sharp teeth marks. Not so long dead.

Even bones are thirsty.

Sarel-girl walks with me, hand on my neck, fingers gripping tight.

I follow Bird-legs-boy to water.

MUSA

❖ ❖ ❖

31

Two days, out and back, and they hadn't found a single drop.

The landscape changed as they moved across the desert. Parched soil gave way to cracked clay, and swaths of grassland dwindled to sparse clumps of low-lying shrubs. The wind scoured the ground as they walked, whipping grit into their eyes.

If he hadn't felt the water, buzzing at the base of his skull, Musa would have given up, would have lain down in the shade of the kennel while his body failed, grateful at least to die without chains.

But he *could* feel it. Right underneath his feet and stretching wide, all around them. So much water, it made his throat ache with hope. It was just nowhere he could get to it.

On the third day, in the middle of a sea of rippled sand, they drained the last of the bladders. Sarel tucked it away in the bottom of her satchel and handed Musa an aloe spear. He sucked at the gel, his throat gagging at the bitter taste.

A rumbling in the distance made Musa stop and whip his head around. For one terrible moment, it sounded just like the dust-clogged engine of Sivo's jeep. But it was only clouds, building in the distance. Right then, it seemed almost worth it to risk a storm, to chance the lightning, if he could feel a few drops of rain fall onto his tongue.

They kept walking, even when the sun was at its highest, even though cramps wracked his belly. Musa walked with a hand pressed to his stomach, the other clamped around the dowsing sticks that trailed in the dirt behind him. He couldn't eat. His body didn't want food if it couldn't have water.

Sarel's steps grew listless, her eyes glazed. Her chin dropped to her chest. The dogs padded limply beside her, panting. Their tongues lolled to the side, heads hung low. Bheka whined with each step. And

Icibi limped, struggling to keep up with the rest of the pack.

High above, a vulture glided, his shrieks jangling on the hot winds.

Chakide's ears pricked and he sniffed the air. He let out an excited bark and ran ahead, his ears flopping up and down with each long stride.

Sarel shouted after him, her voice climbing higher and higher the farther away he ran. Musa's hand flew up to cover his head.

Did she have to scream like that?

Straight ahead, he could just make out the shape of a small puddle. The sun glinted off its slick surface. Chakide stood by the edge, his tail swiping proudly side to side, water dripping off his jowls.

Nandi trotted up to the edge and sniffed, the rest of the pack close behind her. Her tail went stiff and her hackles shot up. She sank her teeth into Chakide's ruff and dragged him away.

Musa squinted. He didn't understand. Why was Nandi being so rough with her pup? And then he saw it. On the far side of the puddle, the body of a bloated hyena lay half in, half out of the water. Flies swarmed all over the rotting carcass.

Nandi whipped around, her tail to the bad water, her teeth bared in a snarl. Slowly the pack backed away, whining, their eyes glassy, tongues licking their dusty snouts.

Running up beside Nandi, her arms flapping to shoo the dogs away, Sarel screamed, "Get back! Get back!"

She fell to her knees beside Chakide, hooking one arm around his neck and stuffing her other hand into his mouth.

"We've got to make him throw it up. Musa, help me!"

Chakide squirmed out of her grasp and ran a few steps away, tail between his legs.

"Help me!" Sarel yelled.

Musa shuffled over and grabbed Chakide by the hips while Sarel shoved her hand down the dog's throat, her face slick with sweat and her lips drawn in a tight white line.

After the third try, Sarel let Chakide go and slumped to the ground.

"It's not working — it's not working!"

Sarel wiped off her hands, took a quavering

breath, and called Nandi to her side. "We've got to get him home."

They hadn't gone half a mile when Chakide began to whine. He retched, his spine curving at a painful angle as his stomach seized. But nothing came up, and his pace slowed, each step stiff.

The pack stopped. Sarel and Musa stood on either side of the dog, hands cradling his head and shoulders. Finally, Chakide's hind legs gave out and he yipped in pain and confusion.

The pack circled around where he sat, panting. They paced, back and forth, in and out. Nandi stood over her pup, licking his ears, sniffing his nose, whining deep in her throat. And then Chakide rolled onto his side, tongue lolling in the dust, his ribs fluttering like a stunned bird.

Musa hefted the shovel and walked a few yards away. He began to dig, thrusting the shovel into the brittle soil, lifting and scattering the dirt. There wasn't any reason why he should find groundwater there, in the spot where Chakide had fallen. But he couldn't sit and watch the dog suffer. His head pounded. His muscles felt like they were ripping apart. He dug a hole in the dirt, the dull shovel barely biting into the sandy soil.

A choked, inhuman sound brought him back, sent him stumbling over the mounds of dirt that surrounded his meager hole. Chakide's body had gone still. His eyes were empty, his jowls slick with foam.

Nandi lay beside her pup, licking his ears and nudging his limp body with her nose. Beside Nandi, Sarel doubled over, pressing her forehead to the ground as silent sobs shuddered through her.

The dogs looked from Musa to Sarel, from Chakide to Nandi. Whipping desert winds snatched thin whines from their throats and tossed them up to the indifferent sun.

While Sarel lay in the dust, clinging to Nandi, Musa finished his digging. He chipped away at the edges, widening the hole until it was big enough to fit Chakide's body, curled into a ball, as if he were only sleeping.

Sarel didn't watch while Musa dragged the dog's limp form across the dirt and lowered him into the ground. But Nandi stood and came to peer down at the unmoving body of her pup. The sun began to tilt westward as Musa filled in the hole.

"Sarel," he said as he tamped the earth over Chakide's grave, "let's go home."

Wiping her bloodshot eyes with the backs of her hands, Sarel stood. She swayed, and a pair of dogs sidled up next to her. She rested her hands on their shoulders, steadying herself. Sarel looked at Musa then, and at the small mound of freshly turned dirt.

"Thank you," she mumbled. She knelt and laid her hand on the grave, closing her eyes while she sucked in a ragged breath. She drew a stone out of her pocket, smooth and white with a black vein through its center, and pressed it into the sandy earth.

Musa held out his hand and Sarel grabbed hold, dragging herself up. She didn't let go all the way home.

SAREL

✤ ✤ ✤

32

Sarel woke, shivering. The warm body that usually slept in the curve of her ribs was missing. She sat up, blinking the sleep from her eyes.

Nandi stood at the edge of the kennel, staring into the distance, her ears pricked forward.

Sarel pulled herself to her feet. She didn't want to walk anymore. Not without Chakide. Not without even a single drop of water to drink.

She squatted down beside Nandi and wrapped her arms around the dog's barrel chest.

Behind her, Musa struggled to sit up. Deep circles bruised the skin under his eyes.

"Come on," he said. "We have to try."

Musa wavered to his feet, tucked his hands under Sarel's arms and tugged upward. A moan slipped past her lips, but Sarel stood while Musa settled her satchel across her shoulder.

Sarel locked Bheka and Icibi in the kennel for the day. They were so weak, and she couldn't bear the idea of losing another dog to the desert. They scratched at the kennel door and pawed at the dirt when the pack left without them, their howls boring into Sarel as she walked away.

Musa trudged beside Sarel, his skin sallow and limp. He looked almost as bad as the first day she'd seen him, parched and bruised and skittish as a cornered animal.

After only an hour of walking, the dowsing sticks fell from Musa's hands. When neither of them stooped to pick them up again, they turned toward home. The day was blistering hot, and the dogs whined through every breath.

Sarel's body felt like it had been stuck with a dozen thorns. She told herself, if this was the end, at least she would get her dogs home. They could rest in the shade; she could kneel between her parents' graves, and lie one last time on the cool grotto stones.

When they came to the riverbed, the pack turned west, following the dust-clogged bedrock homeward. They walked in the belly of the dry river, its trough wide enough for the pack to go side by side. The cut bank rose as high as Sarel's shoulder, the roots of shriveled shrubs dangling over the edges. The watermarks that lined the bank were tinged a greenish white, just like the steep sides of the little hill behind the homestead.

A layer of thin, flat clouds muted the sun for a moment. Sarel felt Nandi stiffen under her hand. The dog turned to look back the way they had come, ears pricked and muscles taut. And then the stones lining the riverbed beneath them began to rattle.

A growl rose deep in Nandi's throat.

Sarel scanned the bank above, her eyes fixing on a sickle bush, whose branches bent low, reaching for the long-gone current.

"Go!" she shouted, slapping the rumps of the dogs within her reach. She grabbed Musa's hand and yanked him over to the cut bank. "Up! Up! Nandi, Thando, Ubali—up!"

They scrambled up, raining pebbles and chunks

of clay onto the bedrock. Nandi was the last to go, and she cleared the cut bank in a single leap, burrowing under the branches and crawling, her belly low to the ground.

They were barely settled behind a loose screen of leaves, ten dogs and two thin, dirt-smothered children, when a burst of pebbles spat from around the bend in the dry riverbed and a jeep rattled toward them.

Four men rode in the open air, their skin dark as silted mud, each with a red cloth knotted at the throat or wrist or temple.

"Sivo," Musa whispered.

Nandi's lips curled up in a warning snarl and Sarel clapped a hand over the boy's mouth.

Thorns pressed into skin and pierced the tender pads of paws already worn raw; dots of blood welled up to the surface. The pack lay silent and still until the dust settled to the riverbed again. Sarel lifted her hand away and Musa squirmed out from under the thorny branches.

"He found me." Musa stared after the fading cloud of dust. "I don't know how he found me."

Sarel wiggled out from under the bush and stood,

checking each of her dogs for thorns. The rush of energy that had come with the fear was draining out of her, leaving her more tired than before.

"Sarel, what do we do?"

She scrambled down the cut bank and up the opposite side. She spoke quickly, to cover the quaver in her voice. "We go back home for Bheka and Icibi." Sarel looked away from her listless dogs, from Musa's terrified face. She had failed them. All of them.

"We leave. And we never come back."

MUSA

✤ ✤ ✤

33

The dry river forked a kilometer east of the home-stead. Tire tracks patterned like snakeskin bit into the dust, turning south.

"They went the wrong way?"

Sarel nodded, but the frown didn't leave her face. "They might be back. We still have to go." To the west, the little hill was a hazy smudge on the horizon, the homestead still too far away to see.

"But we can take a minute"—Sarel winced as she swallowed—"to rest. We won't get very far if we don't rest."

They heard Bheka and Icibi's sharp warning barks long before the homestead came into view.

A growl rumbled through Nandi's chest. The coarse hair along her spine stood on end. The dogs shifted until Sarel was at their center. Ubali trotted out in front of Musa and pressed his body into the boy's legs, herding him back within the pack's protective circle.

Musa let himself be led, but he never took his eyes off the tall, thin figure waiting a few paces away from the kennel.

"Brother," Dingane said, his voice hovering in the space between them. "I found you."

Musa didn't answer. He couldn't.

Dingane started toward him, but the dogs snarled, bristling. Dingane stopped, and his hands fell to his sides. A beetle leaped away from the ground in front of him, snapping its wings together in a clattering hiss.

Musa wanted to run to his brother and weep with relief. He wanted Dingane to suffer like he had suffered all those weeks, alone and afraid. He wanted both, and neither, so Musa only stood and stared, swaying to keep upright.

"I ran away, when Sivo came back that night without you. I left the Tandie. For good. I stole a water jug." Dingane held the empty plastic jug in the air, his teeth flashing as a smile started, then collapsed, on his lips.

"And you think they just let you go? You think they didn't follow you?" Musa waded through the pack of dogs and stalked past his brother. "You led them right to us."

"No—it's not like that," Dingane called after him, palms outstretched. "I swear. I came to find you. Musa, you have to believe me—"

"If you want to help, you should go away," Musa shouted over his shoulder, his voice breaking. "Just go away!"

Sarel put an arm around Musa and pulled him into the kennel.

Dingane's mouth worked in surprise. He settled onto the dirt beside the fire ring.

Sarel peeled back the tough outer skin of an aloe spear and laid it down beside Musa, who had curled up on his sleeping mat, his back to his brother. "Musa, eat this. Rest. But then we have to go. We can't stay here."

Nandi followed Sarel as she left the kennel and latched the rest of the dogs inside with Musa.

Sarel's eyes flicked to Dingane's face and then away, to the far end of the yard. "You heard him. Go away." She limped along the path to the grotto.

Dingane arranged twigs and wisps of grass in the center of the stones. He took a flint out of his pocket and struck it until a spark caught in the dry grass. He blew, and the flame crackled to life.

"Musa, I never thought the Tandie would hurt you. When Umama got sick, I didn't know what to do. I couldn't take care of you both. They promised they would get medicine for her, if you could find a little water for them. I never thought they would take you and lock you up."

Dingane's shoulders twitched as he tossed a handful of twigs onto the fire.

"I never thought they would just let Umama die."

A plume of smoke wove through the air between them.

"When I heard you had run away, I decided to find you. I snuck into Sivo's room. There were old maps pinned up all over the walls. Maps of lakes and rivers that dried up years ago.

"And I saw this place: a big underground lake

with no sign of water anywhere for miles around. Sivo had marked the spots he'd already checked with big red *X*s—and this was one of them. But I thought maybe he missed something. Maybe after everything else was gone, the water deep underground might still be there. And why would he come back if he'd already checked here?"

Musa stuck the aloe spear in his mouth. He winced as the slimy liquid slid down his throat. He didn't care how bad it tasted. It was wet. It was almost water.

"I knew you would find this place. I knew you'd hear a stretch of water this big from miles away. And I thought I could help you. I may not be able to hear the water like you, but Umama taught me to use the sticks too. Did you know that, Musa?"

But Musa still didn't answer. Dingane rummaged in his pack and pulled out a handful of limp tubers. He draped them over the warm rocks to bake.

"I know that when the sticks swing together, I'm standing right at the edge of it. And I know that if I turn and walk away from that spot and count the number of steps it takes before the sticks swing back, I can figure out how far down the water is.

"But that"—his arm stretched long, pointing toward the desert to the south—"that water is deep. While I waited for you today, I kept dowsing right up to the edge, turning and walking away again, and the sticks never swung back.

"If we worked together, I bet we could find a place where it wasn't so deep. We could help each other. Musa, I think Umama would have wanted us to help each other."

Musa didn't move, didn't show any sign that he was listening. But he was. All day, all he had wanted was to stop moving, to lie down. And now his mind wouldn't stop, wouldn't let him rest.

Dingane said that when the sticks swing backwards, that's how you know how far down the water is. And Sarel had said that if there was water anywhere around here, it would be right there, in plain view, beneath the long taproots of the sweet thorn trees.

When Musa had been practicing with his new dowsing sticks, they had swung backwards at the base of the little hill. Not more than one step away from the steep hillsides.

Musa sat up.

That was where the water came up near the surface. Under that little hill. It didn't make any sense, digging for water on top of a hill. But nothing made sense anymore. His mother was gone. His brother had betrayed him. The Tandie were back, and if they caught him they'd never let him go again.

Sarel and Nandi limped back to the kennel. The girl's cheeks were damp, her eyes red and bloodshot.

"Time to go," she said, struggling to lift her satchel onto her shoulder. Sarel swayed, her head bobbing on her neck and her eyelids sagging.

Musa shook his head and helped her down to her own sleeping mat. "Rest, just for a minute. I have to check something."

If he was going to try this, it had to be now. And if he didn't try, they were going to die out there, all of them. Musa left the kennel, Nandi close at his heels. Dingane stood and began to follow him, but Musa shook his head and walked away from his brother.

The other dogs didn't move from the kennel floor, but their eyes followed Musa as he hefted the shovel and began picking his way across the homestead.

Musa and Nandi clambered down into the dry riverbed, following its cut banks straight to the base of the hill. Every step burned in his legs. Every breath scraped through his lungs.

When Musa reached the top of the little hill, he slid between the trees, looking for a spot to begin. The ground was pocked with divots, places where rainwater had pooled and sunk through the porous rock below, the tunnels widening bit by bit, year after year. Maybe there was one that was big enough for the blade of the shovel to fit through, large enough to lower a bucket down and back up, brimming with water.

Musa plunged the shovel into the sunken earth. The dull blade bit into the ground with a *thunk* and the dirt hissed down the hillside as he tossed it out of the way.

Nandi lay beyond the reach of the thorns, her ears pricked forward, eyes focused below on her sleeping pack.

Musa dug until his palms were red and throbbing, until he could barely lift the shovel. Every few breaths, the back of his throat would close in on itself, and he would gasp and sputter until his lungs opened to the air again. His muscles cramped and knotted. He was tired of shoveling, tired from weeks of hard travel, tired from months of abuse and neglect.

The sound of movement below reached his ears. Sarel was up, gathering their things, preparing to leave. He was out of time. Did he really think he could tunnel down through a whole hillside, weak as he was? Musa thrust the shovel into the wall of the pit he had dug and carved out a step. He climbed up and out. The fading sun was glaring, shining red across the flat plain.

Suddenly, Nandi's head shot up and swiveled to the east. She barked, loud, a throaty warning with a high-pitched edge of fear that lifted the hair on Musa's arms. Outside the kennel, the dogs were circling Sarel, tails up, hackles up, all pointing south.

Musa followed their gaze to where four men approached, the desert air blurring the outline of their bodies. Even from a distance, Musa could see their red bandannas and the rifles strapped to their backs as clearly as if they stood beside him.

The Tandie were here. He was too late.

The ground seemed to shift beneath him, and his fingers scrabbled against the gummed bark of the sweet thorn tree beside him.

Musa sidled behind the trunk. Sivo hadn't seen him yet. He could still slip down the other side of the hill and disappear into the desert.

No one would ever find him.

SAREL

✣ ✣ ✣

34

She should run.

But she was so tired.

The men sauntered onto the homestead, guns slung over their shoulders, sweat-soaked red cloths cinched tight.

It was just like before when Sarel had watched through a curtain of heat and dust and waving desert grasses, watched bullets throw the bodies of her father and then her mother to the ground. When the blades of the windmill slashed in lazy circles through billowing clouds. When the dogs in her father's kennel clawed at the chainlink, barking, snarling, digging to get out.

Sarel's nostrils flared, and the wind shifted, washing the smoke of Dingane's fire across her face. She blinked, clearing her eyes of the stinging, swimming tears. She blinked again, and the last wisps of memory fled from her vision.

The dogs pressed in all around her, hackles raised and growls rumbling through their chests. Where was Nandi? Sarel sank her hands into the ruffs of the dogs on either side of her, holding them back from the men with the guns.

"Where is Musa?"

Sivo. That's what Musa called him.

"Where is my dowser?" Sivo slung the rifle over his head and waved it between Sarel and Dingane. Behind him, the other men leveled their rifles at the snarling dogs.

Why didn't the dogs just leave? They might make it. They might. Sarel tried to pull them back, but they were too strong. "Go!" she whispered. "Ubali, Bheka, Thando, get back—run!" Snarls pulled their lips up over their teeth. Where was Nandi? Why had any of them bothered to survive, if it was all going to end like this?

Dingane stepped into the space between the Tandie and the bristling pack, his hands raised high in the air.

MUSA

❖ ❖ ❖

35

Dingane stood in front of Sivo, his bare chest centered on the barrel of Sivo's gun.

"No," Musa whispered. He stepped around the tree. "Don't shoot!" he yelled, pitching his voice to carry down the steep sides of the little hill and across the dry river.

The Tandie turned toward the sound, squinting up at him. Sivo lowered his gun and held a hand up in warning.

While everyone watched Musa pick his way through the trees, Dingane crept around behind Sivo. His eyes flicked up once, to his brother, and then he lunged for the rifle. Sivo threw him off as if he weighed nothing at all. He raised the rifle up to his eye.

"Dingane!" Musa cried.

The *crack* of the gun ripped across the homestead. Dingane's head whipped back and his body crumpled to the ground.

Musa screamed. He ran, stumbling, tripping in the dirt pocked with holes, careening down the side of the little hill. His feet slipped on the scree and he smacked the dirt with a force that stole the air from his lungs.

The ground beneath him buckled.

And then he was sliding, tumbling through rocks and dirt and whipping tree roots. He was falling.

Falling into darkness.

Musa twisted in the air as he fell. Above, the sky was like a blue hole punched out of the earth. A hole in the shape of a ragged oval. A shape like the curve and flex of his mother's hand closing over his own and lifting the dowsing sticks into place.

SAREL

✦ ✦ ✦

36

Sarel couldn't take her eyes off Dingane's leg, twisted beneath him. It looked so painful. She wanted to reach out and straighten it.

A rumble shook the ground beneath her feet, and Sarel turned to see a giant cloud of dust boiling up into the air where the little hill had been.

Nandi burst through the cloud, ears back, baying.

"No," Sarel cried. "Nandi, get back—go!"

But Nandi didn't listen.

A sob broke through Sarel's lips and her grip on Ubali's ruff slackened. He lunged at the man with the gun pointed at her.

Crack.

Ubali yelped. His body was flung backwards as a bullet sank into his chest. Sarel scrabbled to her knees, throwing her arms around Ubali's limp form.

"No!" She was screaming now. "No—get back!"

Crack.

Buttu slumped at her feet, crying piteously as he gnawed at a bullet sunk into his hip. The rest of her pack swarmed in chaos, half snarling and circling the intruders, the other half whining, nudging warm, brown bodies that leaked hot blood onto the earth.

Blood beat at Sarel's temples and her hands clenched into fists. Her mouth opened in a rattling shriek. Sarel ran to the campfire and grabbed a flaming branch. She threw it. Threw it at the men who had come again, come with their guns and their anger and their blood-red flags. She hefted another branch in each hand and ran at them, swiping the flames through the tall grasses and hurling the fiery torches over her head.

Sivo turned his gun on her then, raised it to his eye and sighted down the long black barrel.

Crack.

The bullet shot into the sky, the sound echoing through the smoky air.

Sarel watched Sivo fall. Watched Nandi lunge from behind and sink her jaws into the skin at his throat. Watched her shake once in midair, snapping the life out of her prey in a single, powerful twist.

A gust of wind fanned the grasses and swept the flames across the ground. One second, only a few clumps of grass burned, and the next, everything was smothered in smoke-belching fire. Hot winds whipped across the homestead, and the blades of the old windmill sliced through the black clouds.

The Tandie turned and ran, sprinting to keep ahead of the surging flames. Sarel watched, backing away from the fire until she saw them fall. Backing up, waiting to be sure they didn't get up again.

"Nandi! Come!" Sarel shrieked, choking on the smoke and fanning the air in front of her face. She ran, the dogs pressing close beside her. Halfway there, Buttu crumpled. Flames skipped from one clump of brown grass to another, inches from where he lay, yelping in pain. Nandi lunged back, grabbing Buttu's ruff in her teeth and dragging him away from the fire.

"Nandi!" Sarel screamed as she ducked down the stairs. The dogs leaped down into the grotto, spinning to bark at the smoke that billowed down the stairs after them.

Finally, Nandi backed down into the tiny room, her hind legs straining against the stones, her spine arched, her teeth still clamped into Buttu's fur. A trail of blood followed them down the stone-studded stairs.

"Down," Sarel shouted. "Down!"

She grabbed Nandi around the neck and pulled her to the floor. What was left of the pack huddled against the curved wall. The dogs lay with their bellies pressed to the ground, eyes watching the smoke sifting into the room, noses twitching and lips peeled back in rumbling growls.

Sarel ducked her face under her arm and closed her eyes while the whole world above burned.

SAREL

❖ ❖ ❖

37

When the smoke cleared, when the heat flashing down the grotto stairs faded, Sarel felt her way aboveground. She crawled on her hands and knees, her eyes stinging, her throat ragged and sore.

Everything was black for miles around. The air glowed orange. The haze the fire had left behind clung to everything it touched.

The dogs pressed tight against her as she stumbled past her parents' graves, her eyes skittering away from the charred bodies scattered beyond the kennel.

Where was Musa?

SAREL

❖ ❖ ❖

38

Sarel looked across the dry river, to where half of the little hill had fallen in on itself, leaving a blunt cliff jutting into the air. The rest was gone.

From a dim corner of her mind, from a time before the smoke and the guns and the blood, from a time when they had simply walked hand in hand across a slab of pale stone, her mother's voice prodded:

Rainwater tunnels through porous rock, like sandstone or limestone, until it is brittle as a sun-bleached bone; until one day the ground falls away, causing a sinkhole, a yawning pit in the ground that lays bare the world beneath.

A sinkhole.

It was from there that she had heard Musa shout, from there that Nandi had come running. Sarel limped toward it, her lungs wheezing with every step. A few sweet thorn trees still perched high on the cliff, the long taproots dangling in the air before her. The dogs scrambled around her, hopping from rock to rock, their noses high, sniffing.

And then she stopped, tilted her head, and listened. She heard a sound that made no sense. A sound that her smoke-hazed mind couldn't place. A sound like ripples of water lapping up against the sides of the grotto pool.

Sarel climbed over the last rock and stared down into a shadowed cavern. Nandi leaped up beside her, her paws sending grit raining down into the darkness. The pieces hit bottom with the unmistakable sound of pebbles plinking into water.

Nandi barked, a high-pitched yip, her tail thwacking against Sarel's legs.

"Sarel?"

Her jaw fell open and she shaded her eyes with both hands, peering into the glinting dimness below.

"Musa?"

His voice echoed against the cliff walls. "I'm down here!"

Sarel leaned over the edge, gasping as waves of relief rolled through her. Musa stood on a rock ledge that sloped down into water, which began as a shy turquoise and turned dark as midnight as it deepened. He stood with his hands reaching up toward her, drops of water running between his fingers, over the pink scars at his wrists and down his skinny arms.

He had done it.

He had found the water.

NANDI

❖ ❖ ❖

39

Wind comes. Blows fire scent away. Brings dust from here, from there.

Autumn scent.

Water scent.

Bird-legs-boy carves steps down, down. Down to water under ground.

No more thirsty pups.

Sarel-girl kneels in fire-black dirt, drips water over green things, growing. Pups sniff under her fingers, noses in dirt.

Sarel-girl pulls pups into her arms. Lifts face to wide sky. Makes laughter sound of wood hoopoe bird.

Khee-hee-ee khee-hee-aa-aa-aa.

ACKNOWLEDGMENTS

❖ ❖ ❖

I couldn't have written this book without the love and support of a few dozen wonderful people. First, to my family and friends who have cheered me on and celebrated with me every step of the way, thank you!

My writing was transformed through my studies at Vermont College. I am grateful to the wonderful faculty, staff, and students, and of course my brilliant classmates. Thanks to the workshop group who took a sparse setting and spare character sketch and helped me uncover the rich story beneath: Margaret Bechard, Maha Addasi, Kristin Derwich, Kate Hosford, Cordelia Jensen, and Matt Smith. And of course, my deepest gratitude goes to my exceptional faculty advisors:

Julie Larios, Cynthia Leitich Smith, Franny Billingsley, and Shelley Tanaka.

I am so lucky to have found my fabulous agent, Ammi-Joan Paquette, and the effusive EMLA family.

As for my first readers, who are all excellent writers and excellent friends, my sincere thanks (and the hopes that I can be half as helpful in return) go to Anna J. Boll, Caroline Carlson, Tiffany Crowder, Kristin Derwich, Anna Drury, and Meg Wiviott.

Thanks also to the scholarship committee, who first sent this story to Jeannette Larson and her editorial team. I am grateful to everyone at Houghton Mifflin Harcourt who has worked to turn my manuscript into this beautiful book. And thank you, Reka, for believing in this story from the beginning. Your expertise and guidance has been invaluable.

Thanks to Kathi Appelt, Franny Billingsley, and Rita Williams-Garcia for their generous praise.

And finally, thank you, Whitney, for bringing laughter and love into my life every day.